Star
OF
Deltora
SHADOWS OF THE
MASTER

ALSO BY EMILY RODDA

SHADOWS OF THE
MASTER

EMILY RODDA

An Omnibus Book from Scholastic Australia

Teachers' notes for the *Star of Deltora* series are available from www.scholastic.com.au

Omnibus Books
175–177 Young Street, Parkside SA 5063
an imprint of Scholastic Australia Pty Ltd (ABN 11 000 614 577)
PO Box 579, Gosford NSW 2250.
www.scholastic.com.au

Part of the Scholastic Group
Sydney . Auckland . New York . Toronto . London . Mexico City .
New Delhi . Hong Kong . Buenos Aires . Puerto Rico

First published in 2015.
Text and graphics copyright © Emily Rodda, 2015.
Cover artwork copyright © Marc McBride, 2015.
Cover images copyright © iStock.com / bikerboy82; m-imagephotography.
Cover type by blacksheep-UK.com.
Design and graphics by Kate Rowe.

National Library of Australia Cataloguing-in-Publication entry

Author: Rodda, Emily, author.
Title: Star of Deltora : Shadows of the Master / Emily Rodda.
ISBN: 978 1 74299 062 0 (paperback)
Series: Rodda, Emily, Star of Deltora ; 1.
Subjects: Fantasy fiction, Australian.
Dewey Number: A823.3.

Typeset in Palatino.
Printed and bound by Hung Hing, China.

10 9 8 7 6 5 4 3 2 1   15 16 17 18 19 20/ 0

CONTENTS

1 - The Master of the Staff

The Isle of Tier floated in a faint drift of mist, an emerald rimmed with black on a silver sea. Wide-winged birds wheeled above it but did not land. Great turtles cruised lazily over the hidden fangs of rock that edged its shore. The sun slipped a little lower in the cloudless sky.

In his jewel-studded cavern at the centre of the island, the King of Tier stirred. Shadows flitted around him, eager to do his will. He gestured, and the goblet at his side filled with dark red wine.

Drinking, the King gazed at the crystal fountain he had caused to appear in front of his throne. Shining bubbles floated up from the depths, escaped the water and drifted into the air. As each one broke with a soft, musical chime, a tiny blue bird emerged from it and took wing.

Already a bright cloud of fluttering blue specks

1

had risen to the roof of the cavern, and birdsong of heartbreaking sweetness was mingling with the chimes of the vanishing bubbles.

The sight and sounds were as pleasant as the King had hoped they would be, but he frowned as he sipped his wine. The uneasiness that had been growing within him for days had not become less, and no beauty could relieve it.

Troubling memories he had thought long buried were stirring in his mind. They were rising to the surface, not merrily like the bubbles in the fountain, but slowly and horribly, like dead things drifting up from the ooze of the sea floor into the light.

The King shut his eyes, but pictures still flickered behind his eyelids—pictures from a time long gone. He saw a dawn sky that was as dark as midnight. He saw black clouds rimmed with red tumbling in from the north. He saw the waters of Del harbour churned to foam by a howling wind, and ships swaying and straining at anchor. He saw a tall woman standing braced against the gale in the stern of a ship moored at the dock.

The woman was peering into the darkness of the shore as if she was looking for someone. Her fiery hair flew around her head, her face and cloak were drenched with spray, but she gritted her teeth and did not move.

Mab.

The King of Tier tried to drive the image from

his mind but it would not leave him. And now he could hear the sounds of thunder, groaning timbers and cries of fear that went with the pictures. He could hear the ship's flag—that familiar dark red flag with a large gold 'R' in its centre—snapping in the wind. He could hear waves crashing against the sea wall beside the dock. He could almost feel the sting of spray in his eyes and taste salt on his lips.

He saw the red-haired woman turn as a bearded man in an oilcloth jacket grabbed the rail beside her.

Gripp. Captain Gripp.

'Is the rest of the fleet safely away?' the woman shouted against the wind.

'Aye!' the man bawled back. 'An' if we're to go after them, Mab, it has to be now! The tide turned long ago.'

'We must wait for Sorrel. The Trust Deed—'

'The blockheads probably won't let him have it!' Gripp shouted. 'Face it, girl—they think you're panicking for nothing! Sorrel knew the risk he was taking. I tell you, we've got to—'

There was a fierce gust of wind and the ship bucked. Gripp turned with a furious curse as a fresh-faced young deckhand who had been hesitating behind him lurched forward, crushing him against the rail.

'Mikah!' Gripp roared, when he had recovered his balance. 'What are you playing at, curse you?'

'Sorry, Captain, sir,' the deckhand mumbled, showing the whites of his eyes. 'Sorry, but only—see here! I found a stowaway, hiding in the stores!' With a grunt of effort he heaved forward a ragged, struggling boy he had been dragging behind him.

The boy was dark-haired, dark-eyed, very dirty, and thin as a rail. He looked as if he had been living on the streets, sleeping where he could.

'Don't put me off, Cap'n!' he begged. 'I'll work hard, I swear, if you take me with you! Lean Alice in Anchor Street says the enemy's coming from the Shadowlands. She dreamed it, an' her dreams are always right. She says a bad time's coming that'll last sixteen years or more—an' I don't want to be caught in Del like a fish in a net!'

The tall woman tore her anxious eyes from the darkness and glanced round. The boy seized his chance. He clasped his hands beseechingly.

'I want to be a trader like you, Lady Mab!' he cried over the wind. 'It's all I ever wanted—ask Lean Alice! I want to buy an' sell an' get rich. I want to sail the nine seas an' find all the wonders in the tales—the Isle of Dreams, the Crown of Snakes, the Staff of Tier that cures all ills …'

'If such fables interest you, you are not a trader but a treasure hunter, and will come to no good!' Mab snapped.

Remembering those words, the King of Tier winced. He wondered that he could still see so clearly Mab's face as it had been at that moment—scowling, wet with spray and pale with tension. How was it possible that his memory of a time at least forty years ago could be so clear, so vivid in every detail, when the memories of the recent past were so vague and hard to recall?

He pondered this for a moment, but now that they had begun, the memories of that morning in Del harbour were rising faster and faster, flooding the surface of his mind. He could not resist them—almost, he did not *want* to resist them. He struggled only a little before again surrendering himself to the past.

Once more, thunder growled overhead and salt spray stung his eyes as he saw Mab's frown abruptly change to a grimace of relief. Feet were thudding on the gangplank. A finely dressed young man was boarding the ship, staggering under the weight of a gold-framed painting and a flat wooden box.

Gripp instantly lurched away, bawling orders to his crew.

'Sorrel!' cried Mab, taking the box from the young man's hands. 'Thank the stars! And you brought the portrait too!'

'I could not bear to leave it for the enemy to find,' Sorrel panted, lowering the heavy painting to rest on the deck as the gangplank was rapidly shipped and the rattling of anchor chains began. 'Mab, my father and the other traders still do not believe in the invasion. I had to pretend to agree with them, then steal the Deed and the portrait while their backs were turned.'

'Dimwitted fools!' Mab spat. 'Do they not believe

the evidence of their own eyes?'

Sorrel swallowed. 'The harbour master is not as sure as they are, but he says we are wrong to flee. He says that if the enemy is coming indeed, we should stay and fight.'

He glanced back at the dock, clearly torn.

'Zandalin is an honorable man,' Mab said grimly, 'but he does not know Deltora's history as I do. If the Shadow Lord is coming, it means that the king's magic has been broken. Anyone who tries to fight the invasion openly is doomed. The king himself will have gone into hiding by now, if he has any sense.'

She regarded Sorrel's troubled young face, and her frown deepened. 'As I said in the Traders' Hall, the enemy's first act will be to cut Del off from the outside world by burning every ship in the harbour. I make no excuses for saving the Rosalyn fleet from that fate—it is no more than my duty. But if it helps you, Sorrel, I am certain that preserving our ships will in the end prove to be a greater service to Deltora than anything else we might do.'

Sorrel hesitated, biting his lip, then nodded. 'Who do we have here?' he asked abruptly, eyeing the ragged boy, who had begun struggling in the grip of his captor again the moment the gangplank had been shipped.

'A new member of the crew, it seems,' said Mab, watching the menacing sky. 'Just as well. We are shorthanded. Many of our regular men refused

Gripp's call—the dolts think they will be safer in port than at sea in this weather. The boy has more sense. Mikah, let him go! What is your name, boy?'

The boy's dark eyes were sparkling. 'My name's Larsett,' he said, and his sharp, dirty face broke into a cheeky grin. 'But on the street, they call me "Dare".'

'Do they indeed?' Mab raised her eyebrows, but a smile twitched at the corners of her own lips.

'Who's that?' the boy asked, pointing at the painting Sorrel had brought on board, a portrait of a stern, beautiful woman.

Mab glanced at him. 'That is the first Trader Rosalyn. It is thanks to her that the Rosalyn fleet exists, and it is thanks to the Trust Deed she left behind her that I am the Trader Rosalyn today, the last in a long, long line.'

'Not the last, I hope!' Sorrel put in, then looked aghast at his own daring.

Astonishingly, Mab threw back her head and laughed. 'Indeed, Sorrel!' she cried over the wind. 'This day, I hope, we will ensure that the Rosalyn line will not end with me, but will continue for centuries to come.'

Above their heads sails billowed and the great ship surged toward the harbour entrance. Mab's laughter died.

'If Lean Alice is right, we will not see Del again for sixteen years or more,' she said. 'The boy here, and Mikah, will be grown men when we return. You will

7

be in your thirties, Sorrel. And I … I will be well past fifty!'

The boy who called himself Dare Larsett gave a shrug. 'We'll be alive,' he said simply. 'That's what counts.'

The King of Tier groaned and opened his eyes. With a mighty effort he forced the memory down. The wraiths around him twined together, advancing and retreating, flickering in agitation.

Larsett, he heard them whispering. *What ails you, Larsett, Master of the Staff?*

Seeking to calm them and himself, the King tightened his grip on the glinting black Staff that stood beside his throne. His mind cleared, slowed, grew still. Briefly he wondered how much the Staff was changing him, and a quiver passed through his body like a cool breeze skimming through long grass. Then he set the thought aside. There was something more important to consider.

Why had that memory returned to plague him? He had been so young, then. It had all been so long ago …

Yet how different his life would have been if he had not sailed with Mab that day! Minutes after the black cloud rolled over Del and covered it, every ship remaining in the harbour had been reduced to charred splinters. But the ships that flew the Rosalyn flag were all at sea by then, on their way to a safe and distant shore.

Few in Del knew of the escape. Those who did know thought they had seen the last of the Rosalyn fleet, and over the years of misery and turmoil that followed the Shadowlands invasion they forgot all about it.

But Mab did not forget her homeland. When word came to her at last that the ancient magic that protected Deltora had been restored and the invader repelled for good, she brought back to Del a trading fleet that was even larger than it had been before. So it was that Del had ships again far sooner than anyone had thought possible. So it was that food could be brought to the hungry people and trade with other lands could quickly begin once more.

And so it was that over the years of rebuilding, Mab became a legend in her own time, though some people still muttered that she would have acted more nobly if she had stayed to face the enemy, and let her ships burn.

The King of Tier shook his head. Mab could not be at the core of his growing feeling of unease. By now Mab must surely be dead, or at least very old and frail. Yet the memories of her on Del's darkest day had come to him. Why?

Coolly this time, and without haste, he searched for meaning. And then he saw it—saw it in the dark, flashing eyes of the young stowaway who wanted to be a trader.

He remembered another pair of eyes, just as dark,

just as sparkling, from a later time—a time much nearer to the present. He remembered a small girl standing on the deck of a brand new ship, beneath a brilliant sky. 'Mother says I must grow up to be a lady, Father!' the girl was declaring, her voice shrill with frustration. 'But I want to be a trader, like you!'

Could it be ...?

Feeling an emotion he had not felt for a very long time, the King set his wine goblet down.

'Something is happening, a long way from here,' he said aloud, his voice cracked and rusty with disuse. 'There is a change. I feel it, and must know more of it. The place is Deltora—the city of Del—far across the Silver Sea. The person is a girl—no, a young woman now. Her name is ... Britta.'

A few slender shadows rushed from the cavern, leaving the rest to whisper by the walls. The King of Tier let his breath go in a deep sigh. Then he picked up his goblet once more and returned to watching his birds.

2 - Britta

Far away, in a poky little shop in the centre of the city of Del, a customer with a face like a fish was shaking her narrow head. 'A *whole* cheese?' the woman was exclaiming. 'Bless me, what are you thinking of, my girl? A good-sized wedge is all I want.' But while her mouth said one thing, her pale eyes, sliding back to the plump little cheese nestled in its basket lined with vine leaves, said quite another.

Standing demurely behind the counter, her dark brown hair properly bound in a knot at the nape of her neck, her decent blue skirt and prim white shirt covered by a starched apron, Britta smiled.

This customer was a stranger. She had never been in the shop before, and was unlikely ever to enter it again. The moment she walked through the door, Britta had decided it was safe to bargain with her. No one who mattered would ever hear of it.

'Oh, of course, madam!' Britta said politely, reaching for the basket. 'You mentioned you had friends coming for supper, so I suddenly thought of this … But actually, it is just as well you have decided against it.'

'Oh?' The woman frowned. 'Why is that?'

'Well, these cheeses are rather special, you see, and this is the last we have,' Britta said, lifting the basket and half-turning as if to put it back on the shelf behind the counter. 'I should really be keeping it for one of our regular customers. We give a jar of our best pickled onions with every whole cheese sold, you know.'

A hand shot out and held the basket fast. 'I have changed my mind,' the woman said. 'Why not? I can afford that cheese, and you are right—it will look well on my supper table.'

With her free hand she drew out her purse. Britta waited, carefully expressionless.

The little bell over the shop door tinkled wildly. Britta cursed in very unladylike fashion under her breath as the door burst open and a hairy, grinning, long-armed creature capered in.

The fish-faced woman shrieked and shrank back, pressing her purse tightly to her chest. Ignoring her, the hairy creature bounded onto the counter and thrust a scrap of paper into Britta's hand.

It was a scrawled note, very short. Britta read it at a glance.

Britta's throat tightened. Was Captain Gripp ill? Had he fallen in his cluttered little cottage and hurt himself?

No. Unconsciously she shook her head. Gripp had plenty of friends in Del harbour. If he needed help, he would hardly have sent his polypan all the way to Britta, in the centre of the city.

'A polypan!' babbled the customer, staring in disgust at the creature chattering and bouncing on the counter. 'I have not seen one of those foul things since the invasion ended! Bless me, what sort of shop *is* this?'

Britta pulled herself together. She stuffed the note into her apron pocket and snatched a lump of strong-smelling toffee from a jar. 'All right, Bosun!' she said sharply, pushing the toffee into the creature's outstretched paw. 'Go home now! Go home!'

The polypan gave a screech and sprang off the

counter. In moments it had shot back through the shop door and was cantering off down the street.

'Ugh!' The woman fanned herself. 'If there is one thing I cannot abide, it is polypans! Nasty, dirty, thieving beasts! Bless me, I am all of a tremble! I think I had better …' She began to put her coin purse away.

Do not let her go! Britta told herself fiercely. Do not lose the sale! Put everything else out of your mind!

'I am sorry you were startled, madam, but Bosun works for one of our oldest customers, and is quite harmless,' she said quickly, reflecting that at least some of those words were true.

Then she had an inspiration. She wrinkled her brow. 'He brought a note, as you saw. Captain Gripp wants …' She paused, bit her lip, and glanced beneath her eyelashes at the cheese in the basket.

'Well, if this Captain Gripp wants *my* cheese, you must tell him his note came too late!' the woman declared shrilly, recovering instantly at the thought that she had a rival for her prize. 'Wrap it well, if you please. And mind you do not forget the pickled onions!'

Soon she was bustling importantly out of the shop, her string bag bulging. Her coin purse was much lighter than it had been before, but clearly she was very well satisfied with her bargain.

So was Britta. She had sold a whole cheese—more cheese than her mother's shop usually sold in a week!

And it was all thanks to a grass basket that had once held eggs, and a few leaves from the vine that grew at the back door. Of course, she had given away a jar of pickled onions to seal the bargain, but that was no loss. Her mother had filled dozens of jars when onions were cheap, and they had sat on the storeroom shelves so long that they seemed to have taken root there.

Still, Britta's elation was already fading as she put the handful of coins into the cash tin and stowed the tin beneath the counter. Shadows had begun crawling among the boxes and barrels on the shop floor almost as if they had slipped through the doorway as her customer marched out. The thought was vaguely disturbing and Britta hastily dismissed it, reminding herself that it was late afternoon, when shadows were to be expected.

The day had almost ended, and thoughts of Captain Gripp's message were plaguing her. She was burning to find out what the old man wanted. She pulled out the note and read it again.

Come at once …

If only she could! But it was impossible to leave the shop unattended, and even after closing time it would be hard to get away without having to answer awkward questions.

She swung round, guiltily crumpling the note in her hand, as her older sister, Margareth, hurried in from the back of the shop, tying an apron around her slim waist.

'I am sorry your break has been so delayed, Britta,' Margareth said in her usual gentle tones. 'I could not come before.'

'How is Mother?' Britta just remembered to ask as she tore off her own apron and quickly edged out from behind the counter so that Margareth could take her place.

'The lavender water eased her headache a little,' Margareth replied. 'She took some broth, and now she is asleep. That will do her good, I am sure.'

She sighed. 'It is the same every year, around this time. If only she could stop brooding about things that are past. If only she could forget!'

Britta's lips tightened. 'Mother will never forget,' she muttered, stuffing her apron heedlessly behind a pile of wooden buckets. 'How can any of us forget, while we still live in Del? While we have to pretend, and lie, and dread the moment when one of our neighbours guesses who we are? We should have moved away— far away—to some place where no one has ever heard of Father, never heard the name Larsett!'

The shadows seemed to stir around her as she spat out the final word—stir, and press eagerly closer. Britta felt their yearning, loving warmth flow through her, but blamed her anger for the heat. Irritably she pressed the back of her hand against her burning cheek.

'If there is such a place,' she added bitterly. 'Perhaps Mother fears there is not, and that is why she keeps to this wretched hole.'

Aware that her sister was staring at her in concern, she strode to the door. She did not mention the fine sum of money in the cash box. Suddenly it made her sick to think that she could have felt triumphant because she had managed to sell a whole cheese to a thrifty housewife. What a grand victory for the daughter of the man who had once been the second most famous trader in Del!

She jerked the door open. The sound of the tinkling bell set her teeth on edge.

'Where are you going?' Margareth cried after her.

'To the harbour,' Britta snapped, too irritated to avoid the question. 'Captain Gripp sent for me.'

She looked back over her shoulder, saw that her sister's eyes had widened in alarm, and felt even angrier. 'I must go!' she said. 'What Mother does not know will not hurt her. Do not wait dinner for me—and do not worry!'

But she knew Margareth *would* worry. She knew Margareth would not have a moment's peace until she returned and the door was safely locked behind her.

The thought made her bolt out into the street without another word. For an instant she stood still, gulping the air that despite its sharp mixture of city odours seemed pure after the stale, grocery-smelling fug of the shop. Then, head down to avoid the eyes of passers-by, she set off in the direction of the harbour, the patched soles of her boots rapping on the cobblestones.

She was walking so fast, and thinking so furiously, that at first she did not hear the call from the other side of the street. Only when the call was repeated did she look up. A young man dressed all in white was plunging across the road towards her, narrowly avoiding a clattering horse-drawn cart.

Jantsy. Britta stopped and waited, shifting impatiently from foot to foot. If Jantsy had finished at the bakery, it was even later than she had thought.

Grinning, Jantsy reached her side, pushing back the lock of thick, honey-coloured hair that had been tumbling over his forehead for as long as she had known him. As always he smelled sweetly of sugar, cinnamon and the good things he baked.

'Britta! What are you doing out and about?' he asked. 'Where are you going?'

'Captain Gripp's. And I cannot stop, Jantsy,' Britta said. 'I cannot stay out too long.'

'I will go with you, then,' the young man said agreeably. 'I have not been to the harbour in an age.'

'Neither have I.' Britta frowned. Her last visit to Captain Gripp's cottage had been on her birthday, a month ago. A lot could happen in a month, especially to a man of Gripp's age.

She began walking again, even faster than before. Jantsy fell into step beside her, his long legs keeping pace with her easily. For a time they went along in companionable silence, and Britta felt herself beginning to relax. With Jantsy, she did not have to pretend. She had told him her family's secret long ago, knowing that he would never betray her.

'Mother does not know where I am going,' she said abruptly. 'If she did, she would get out of bed, no matter how badly she felt, and think of some reason for me to stay at home. She hates me seeing Gripp—hates it!'

'You said Gripp was your father's friend in the old days—sailed with him for many years,' said Jantsy, shrugging. 'No doubt your mother fears he is a bad influence.'

Britta snorted. 'That is ridiculous! I visit Captain Gripp because he is old and in pain and likes to see me. He is perfectly respectable, and he never *mentions* my father!'

Realising that she had raised her voice, she glanced from side to side, caught the eyes of two passing women, and quickly looked down again.

'See how they stare?' she hissed. 'Oh, how I hate this gossiping place! Whenever I go out I feel eyes following every step I take, and today it seems worse than ever!'

Shadows flickered before her eyes, and she felt them pressing against her just as they had in the shop. Her skin prickled. She darted a quick look at Jantsy, but plainly he had noticed nothing.

I am just imagining things, Britta told herself.

19

This is what comes of getting so angry and upset. I am as bad as those people driven mad by slavery in the Shadowlands. They always think they are being watched and followed.

No sooner had the thought crossed her mind than she felt ashamed. She glanced up at the palace of Del, set high on a hill and visible from every part of the city. In olden times, Deltora's royal family had lived there in splendid isolation. Now the palace was a refuge for people damaged in body and mind by the Shadowlands invasion.

It was cruel and stupid to liken herself to those sad, lost souls who even Deltora's king with all his magic could not cure. Her troubles were fleabites compared to what they had suffered. She had been born when the enemy across the mountains had been repelled and had turned his attention to other conquests. In her time, Deltora had always been safe and full of hope for the future.

And yet … what hope did she have for *her* future—the future she had dreamed of all her life? Perhaps it made perfect sense for her to imagine she was being followed. For in a way she *was*. Wherever she went, whatever she did, she was followed by her past.

One day I will escape it, Britta swore to herself. One day … And resisting the impulse to look behind her again, she hurried on.

3 - The *Star of Deltora*

In concern, Jantsy glanced at his companion's knitted brows. 'The neighbours only stare because they know you from the shop, Britta,' he said. 'No doubt they are curious because you, Margareth and your mother live so quietly, and so rarely leave home.'

And because you are beautiful, Britta, he might have added. Because your face is full of life, and your eyes seem to sparkle when you speak. But if these thoughts crossed Jantsy's mind, he knew better than to let them reach his lips.

'They mean no harm,' he said instead.

'They would mean harm enough if they knew that my father was the most hated man in Del,' Britta said bitterly. 'It has been eight years this month since we fled the harbour, Jantsy. Eight *years!* And I am sick of shame and hiding. Sick to death!'

Jantsy did not answer. He just let her anger ride between them till slowly it began to dissolve in the cooling air.

Perversely Britta tried to hold on to it. 'If Mother thinks Gripp is so bad for me, why does she not just forbid me to see him?' she demanded.

'Because she knows you would sneak out and see him anyway,' said Jantsy simply.

Britta frowned, then suddenly burst out laughing. She heard Jantsy laughing with her, and walked on with a lighter heart. There was something very comforting about being with Jantsy.

The day was waning and the light was mellow gold by the time the pair reached the maze of old, narrow streets surrounding the harbour. The harbour district had somehow survived the sixteen years of enemy occupation that had laid so many other parts of the city to waste. Much of it had not needed to be cleared and rebuilt, so it remained as it had always been.

Here, noisy taverns stood on almost every corner. Gaudily dressed sailors jostled in the throngs surrounding street musicians, jugglers and conjurors. The breeze that whipped bright colour into Britta's cheeks and teased strands loose from the tight knot of her hair brought with it the smell and taste of the sea.

Britta slowed a little. Jantsy glanced at her and saw that she was smiling.

'I love being here,' she said. 'Here everyone is too

busy to care about what anyone else is doing. Mother is terrified that I will be recognised by someone who used to know us, but I was very young when we moved away and I look quite different now. Besides, I never go into a shop or talk to anyone except Captain Gripp. Oh, it is glorious to be just a face in the crowd!'

Jantsy nodded cheerfully, but as the girl moved on, her eyes shining, his smile faded a little. Perhaps Britta did enjoy being just a face in the crowd, but he was sure that this was not the only reason for her rising spirits.

More important was the harbour, coming into their sight as the street dipped and broadened. More important were the slap of water against the timbers of the docks, the shouts of people buying and selling, the scents of tea and spices. And most important of all were the tall ships swaying at anchor—the merchant ships that flew with the wind across the wide blue sea and brought the bounty of faraway places to Del.

It is in her blood, thought Jantsy. Margareth is her mother's daughter, but Britta is her father's, whatever she says and whatever she thinks.

It came to him that this was probably at the heart of Britta's mother's objection to Captain Gripp. It was not the influence of the *man* Maarie feared, but the influence of the harbour itself.

And Jantsy suddenly found that he feared it too.

He caught a stealthy movement from the corner of his eye and looked round quickly. A thin-faced woman with an embroidered shawl over her head was staring fixedly at Britta and making strange signs in the air with her hands. Her long, grimy fingers were heavy with rings that flashed in the light.

Jantsy realised with shock that the signs were intended to ward off evil. Assuming that the woman had recognised Britta, he scowled at her and angrily gestured at her to keep back.

'I see what others do not, boy,' the woman said in a low, whispering voice. 'Take care. That young lady does not walk alone.'

'She certainly does not!' Jantsy hissed back, relieved to see that Britta had moved on and had not heard. 'I am with her. And no one will insult her while I can prevent it.'

The woman shrank away from his anger, but still her hands made those strange, busy movements in the air. 'You will learn, my brave fellow!' she spat as he turned to hurry after Britta. 'There will come a time when you will wish you had listened to Lean Alice!'

Telling himself that the woman was mad, Jantsy hurried to catch up with Britta. Just as he fell into step beside her, they turned the last corner and Britta stopped dead, her breath catching in her throat.

Del harbour lay before them, broad and gleaming. At the central dock, a beautiful three-masted vessel was being loaded with stores.

'The *Star of Deltora*,' Britta murmured, her lips barely moving.

A dark red flag with the gold letter 'R' in its centre fluttered at the beautiful ship's stern. Jantsy stared at it. The traders of Del harbour were not part of his world, yet even he knew what that flag meant. It showed that the ship was part of the Trader Rosalyn fleet—the largest merchant fleet in Del.

But eight years ago, he knew, the *Star of Deltora* had flown a different flag. Eight years ago, when it was new, the ship had belonged to Britta's father. It was in the *Star of Deltora* that Dare Larsett had sailed away from Del, never to return.

Jantsy's heart twisted as he looked from the ship to Britta's closed face. Larsett's obsession with the fabled Staff of Tier had led to the loss of the family's fine house on the harbour, the loss of a rich livelihood, the loss of pride and reputation and the loss of a place in the trading community of Del.

But now Jantsy realised that for Britta the greatest disaster of all had been the loss of the *Star of Deltora*. For now he saw, in her bleak eyes, all that the ship had meant to her.

'You were just a child when it was sold.' He blurted the words out in haste, and instantly he wished that he could take them back.

But Britta only nodded, gazing at the ship. 'All I wanted, then, was to be a trader like my father,' she said in a low voice. 'I remember telling him so, standing on the deck of the *Star*, just before he went away.'

She had never mentioned this to Jantsy before.

It was as if the sudden sight of the ship had unlocked a memory that she had kept hidden away, even from herself.

'He said that of course I could be a trader if I really wished it,' she went on. 'We would sail the seas together, he and I, and he would teach me everything he knew. He said he had named the ship *Star of Deltora* because for travellers lost in the night, stars were like beacons in the darkness, guides to be trusted, true and bright and never changing. He said that the *Star* was like that. She would never fail us. She had been built for us and she was our ship—ours forever!'

She shrugged. 'But of course,' she went on in a flat voice, 'as it turned out, Father found something else he cared for more than the *Star of Deltora* ... or anything else.'

In dismay, Jantsy saw the bitterness bubbling within her, tightening her mouth and hardening her eyes.

He had known Britta for years before she told him who her father was. It had happened the first time her mother had caught her bargaining with a customer in the shop, instead of simply taking money for goods in the usual way. There had been a terrible argument, and Britta had appeared at the back door of the bakery her whole body trembling, her eyes huge and burning in her white face.

She had shed no tears—Britta never cried—but her misery had been heartbreaking as clumsily Jantsy tried to comfort her. Still, he had preferred it to this. For an instant he seemed to see dark shapes twining around Britta like smoke. He remembered the thin woman in the street, and shuddered. Then he blinked and the shadows were gone.

'You wanted to see Captain Gripp,' he said steadily. 'And it is getting late ...'

Britta turned to him, away from the sight of the beautiful ship, and nodded.

They made their way along the harbour shore to the huddled little cottage that had become Captain Gripp's refuge after a lifetime at sea. The sun was setting, but the windows of the house glowed with soft light, warm and welcoming.

'You will want to go in alone,' Jantsy said when they reached the low wall that surrounded Gripp's yard. 'He does not know me. I will wait for you here, and walk home with you when you are ready.'

Britta pressed his hand gratefully, and left him sitting on the wall, apparently quite content.

Her feeling that she was being followed suddenly returned, and she could not help looking uneasily over her shoulder before rapping at the cottage door. But all she could see behind her was Jantsy's silhouette perched on the wall, and all she could hear was the sound of Jantsy whistling softly in the dark.

So she knocked. There were thudding sounds inside the cottage, and the door was wrenched open by Bosun, the polypan. To Britta's surprise, Bosun gibbered when he looked out, baring his teeth and springing back as if he was afraid.

'It is only me, Bosun,' Britta said. But Bosun just hooted and bobbed, the hair on the back of his neck standing up like a threadbare ruff. His glassy stare seemed fixed not on Britta, but on something directly behind her. She glanced quickly over her shoulder again, and again saw nothing to fear.

'Britta?' Captain Gripp's voice called. 'Come in, girl! Come in!'

The old man sounded healthy and happy enough. Relieved, Britta stepped into the dim hallway. Shadows crawled around her feet as she closed the door behind her. The polypan screeched, spun round and made for the lighted sitting room, his head down, his hairy knuckles dragging on the floor. Wondering what ailed him, Britta followed.

A kettle simmered on the black stove on one side of the sitting room, but the sagging armchair drawn up to the hearth was empty. Captain Gripp was still sitting in his usual daytime spot by the front window, his padded wooden crutch to hand, a telescope by his side and the whole wonder of Del harbour spread out before him.

'What's got into you, you fool of a creature?' he growled at Bosun, who had leaped onto the deep windowsill and was teetering there, shivering and showing the whites of his eyes. 'Pay no heed to him, Britt. Fleas, I wouldn't be surprised. Come an' sit by me. I've news for you—the best of news!'

'What—what is it?' Britta faltered. Suddenly she felt dizzy. The light in the room seemed dazzling. Grey shapes were flickering before her eyes.

She moved uncertainly towards Gripp's chair and groped for the little wooden stool she always sat on during her visits. The polypan sprang frantically off the windowsill and bolted to the other end of the room.

'Bosun, stop your nonsense!' the old man roared. 'Bring tea! Good an' strong, too, you villain, or I'll have your guts for garters.'

The polypan chattered and whimpered, but at last crept to the stove and began a great clattering with a battered teapot, two enormous mugs and a painted tin tray.

'What is your news, Captain Gripp?' Britta begged, raising her voice over the din. 'Tell me!'

Gripp rubbed his crooked hands together. His chest swelled. 'Mab, the Trader Rosalyn, has decided she's ready to choose her Apprentice! Not before time, either, an' maybe she knows it, because now she's made up her mind she's going at the thing under full sail. She's testing out candidates tomorrow. An' you're in the running, Britta—I've seen to it!'

As Britta gaped at him, he nodded vigorously.

'I've seen to it!' he repeated. 'It's my right as a retired captain of the Rosalyn fleet to sponsor a candidate, an' I did it. Your entry was accepted just about straight off, Britt, near on three weeks ago. I didn't send for you then because—well, I knew your mother wouldn't be too happy with the idea. It's nearly been the death of me, holding on to the news, but I thought it'd be best to spring it on you, like, so you wouldn't be tempted to tell her.'

'Captain Gripp!' Britta croaked. 'I—this is—'

'The testing starts in the Traders' Hall at eight tomorrow morning,' the old man broke in, beaming. 'An' if you're one of the three finalists, Britt, you'll set sail with Mab the next day—in the *Star of Deltora!*'

4 - The Chance

Britta sank down on the stool, staring at Gripp, who was still nodding and grinning like a toy clown with its head on a spring. 'There'll be plenty of competition, Britt,' he said. 'A lot of the big Del traders have daughters the right age, for a start. Slippery as eels, some of them, I daresay. But you'll be a match for them, I'll bet money on it.'

Britta wet her lips. 'Mab would never accept me as her Apprentice, Captain Gripp,' she said huskily. 'Once she finds out who my father is—'

'Ha!' Gripp's shaggy white eyebrows shot up. 'And why should she find out? Unless you tell her, Britt, and a fine fool you'd be to do that!'

'But—'

'A good trader doesn't tell all her secrets—I heard that from Mab's own mouth a thousand times when I was sailing with her,' the old man broke in.

'I put on your entry that you were an orphan, which is half true—or might as well be. I said you were old enough, an' you are—just. I said you were distant kin of mine—an' that's true too, Britt. Except for the kin part, I s'pose, strictly speaking, but friends are as good as family an' I *have* known you since you were born.'

He frowned as Britta buried her face in her hands.

'Now, listen here,' he said, leaning forward and tapping the girl's knee with a crooked finger. 'This is your chance, Britta—your chance to be what you were born to be! It's the one thing I could do for you. Don't you go disappointing me.'

Britta made herself look up. 'I am grateful for what you have tried to do, Captain Gripp,' she managed to say. 'I really am. But truly, even if I went to the Traders' Hall tomorrow, and even if no one realised who I was, how could I hope to do well enough to be a finalist? I have no real trading experience. I have been to no foreign lands. I have not stood on the deck of a ship since I was seven years old ...'

The old man regarded her under his eyebrows, then pulled a folded paper from beneath the tea tray.

'Take a look at this,' he ordered, thrusting the paper at Britta. 'Then tell me you're not as good a candidate as any.'

Numbly, Britta unfolded the paper. It was rubbed and tea-stained, but the words printed on it were still very clear.

Mab, the Trader Rosalyn, calls for candidates to compete for the right to become her Apprentice. Please note the following terms, which are based on the original Rosalyn Trust:

★*Candidates must be female citizens of Deltora aged between 15 and 18 years.*

★*Every candidate must be sponsored by an adult citizen of good reputation.*

★*A basic level of education is required, but experience is not important. Candidates will be judged on character, intelligence, and trading instincts.*

★*On the day of testing, three finalists will be chosen. They will be taken on a trial trading voyage on the finest ship of the line, the **Star of Deltora**.*

★*All finalists will be given trading funds. Provided that in the opinion of the Trader Rosalyn she will bring credit to the Rosalyn fleet, the finalist who brings goods of the highest value back to Del will win the right to be the Trader Rosalyn Apprentice.*

★*Upon the death of the present Trader Rosalyn, her Apprentice will inherit the title, and all the rights and responsibilities this title conveys, including full ownership of the ships of the fleet.*

Entry forms and further details may be obtained from the Trader Rosalyn office.

33

When Britta looked up, she was breathing fast. As Gripp had hoped, the flat, official words of the notice had roused her in a way his encouragement could not.

She knew about the Rosalyn Trust, of course—the story was part of Deltoran folklore. She knew that since ancient times the ownership of the Rosalyn fleet had been passed on by competition, rather than by inheritance. She knew that the strange, hard, powerful woman who had been the original Trader Rosalyn had died without an heir, leaving strict instructions as to how her ships and fortune were to be passed on.

It had never occurred to Britta, however, that the old story might have any meaning for her. At seven, she had wanted nothing more than to sail with her beloved father on the *Star of Deltora*. In the years since, she had assumed that Larsett's disgrace had barred her forever from any contact with the life she would otherwise have chosen.

Now she had seen in black and white that she filled all the requirements of the Rosalyn Trust. She had not been able to stop imagining herself escaping from the dull little shop to sail the wide seas, visit foreign ports, see the wonders she had read about—and trade, without fear, for a living.

And she had been forced to consider that if by some miracle she were to win the contest, the *Star of Deltora* would one day be hers.

The polypan sidled from the stove, two overfull

34

mugs of very black tea clinking together on his tray. By the time he slammed his burden down on the rickety little table by the captain's chair, the tray was flooded and the mugs were half empty, but Britta and Gripp helped themselves without comment. They were both used to Bosun's tea-making style, which was always slapdash even when he was in a good mood.

Britta took a sip. The hot, dark liquid was bitter on her tongue, but it steadied her.

Gripp looked at her keenly. He nodded with satisfaction but did not try to speak to her.

'Fire up another lamp, Bosun,' he growled instead. 'It's pesky dark in here tonight.'

As the polypan did as he was told, and the room brightened, Britta's eyes were drawn irresistibly to the wall opposite the stove. The far end was lined with open shelves crammed with the books of traders' tales she loved but was forbidden to read at home. The end nearer to the window was devoted to glass-fronted cabinets filled with Gripp's souvenirs of his life at sea—oddly shaped shells, the skulls of strange beasts, brass gongs, painted fans, carvings and curios of all kinds.

Ranged on top of the cabinets were exquisitely detailed models of ships, made by Gripp himself in the days before his hands grew knobbly and swollen with what he called 'the pesky arthritics'.

And on a long, low table in front of the cabinets, dominating that corner of the room, was the largest and most intricate model of all—a perfect replica of the *Star of Deltora*.

That, of course, was what wily Captain Gripp had wanted Britta to see. He knew only too well how she felt about the *Star*.

The model was complete in every detail from bow to stern—and not just on the outside, either. One side could be lowered on hidden brass hinges, so that the inside of the ship could be seen as well. Everything was there, from the grand cabins used by the captain and the chief trader to the smaller cabins for other traders and passengers, from the quarters where the crew ate and slept to the holds where goods and supplies were stored.

And Britta knew, because Captain Gripp had told her, that every cabin, every gangway, every hatch and hammock was in its correct place.

Only one thing made the model different from the beautiful ship now being loaded in the harbour. It did not fly the Trader Rosalyn flag, but the white star on deep blue background that Dare Larsett had chosen as his emblem when he left Mab's service to become an independent trader.

The model had been finished just before the ship's first, fateful voyage. In the terrible time after her father vanished, while her mother wept and her sister crept about the silent house on the harbour like a ghost, young Britta had often escaped to Gripp's cottage. There, she was always welcome. And there she could crouch by the model of the ship, so much more fascinating to her than any dolls' house, and take herself on imaginary voyages, making gales with her own breath, and using dried peas for sailors.

She had learned the *Star* inside and out, and with the learning had come love. The ship became a world into which she could escape—her world, free of the fear and confusion that haunted her home.

Those days were long gone.

They had not ended when news came to Del that the haunted Isle of Tier, harmless for hundreds of years, was suddenly alive again—alive and hungry, a danger to every ship that sailed the Silver Sea. They had not even ended when the *Star of Deltora* was found drifting, empty of cargo, with the bleached skeleton of her captain, Mikah, tied to the wheel.

But when the bottle wedged in the hook that had served Mikah for a hand was opened, and the message inside had been read, there was no more play for Britta, or hope for her mother and sister.

Soon every man, woman and child in Del knew the grim story, and finally even those who had claimed at first that it could not possibly be true were forced to believe it. Dare Larsett, the best-loved trader in the city, had found the Staff of Tier and used it to bring the Hungry Isle back to life. Possessed by the Staff, or simply unable to resist the lure of absolute power and everlasting life, Larsett had betrayed his land, his captain, his crew and his ship.

And after that, there was no place for Britta and her family in Del harbour.

Everything was sold to pay Larsett's debts, for he had borrowed heavily to fund his first voyage. The *Star of Deltora* was taken by Mab who, in recognition of Larsett's long and valuable service to the Rosalyn fleet, had lent the money for the ship to be built.

And then Maarie had gathered up her daughters and fled with what little she had left to the centre of the city and a poky shop that she prayed would at least put bread in their mouths. She had been working in a grocery shop when the dashing Dare Larsett first saw her and swept her off her feet. A shop, for her, meant safety—the safety she had known before her marriage, before Larsett had carried her off to the big house on the harbour.

No one knew where Maarie and her children had gone, and few people cared. Compared to the tempest raised by Larsett's disgrace, his family's flight made only a tiny ripple on the surface of harbour life, barely noticed and soon forgotten.

In truth, Maarie had never been part of the Del trading community. Timid and very conscious of her humble beginnings, she had always preferred to stay quietly at home with her daughters while Larsett voyaged to distant lands with Mab and made a fortune for the Rosalyn fleet.

Britta had wept bitterly on leaving her old home, but she had never wept since. It was as if the well of her tears had dried up, leaving an empty hole in the centre of her mind. Sometimes her mother accused her of being hard and uncaring, but Britta knew she was not. She told herself that she simply had no more tears to shed.

Years had passed before she made her way back to the harbour and to Captain Gripp. But return to them she had at last, to be welcomed joyously, and to find everything in the little cottage unchanged. She no longer played games with the model of the *Star*, but she still knew every tiny rope, every winch, sail and corner of the ship.

'The real *Star*'s no different now to what she was at first, from what I hear,' Gripp muttered, watching Britta under his eyebrows. 'Mab didn't change a thing.'

And in that moment, Britta threw caution to the winds. She tore her eyes from the model ship and looked up at the old man staring at her so anxiously.

'I will be at the Traders' Hall tomorrow,' she said. 'How can I resist?'

'Hooroar!' Captain Gripp bellowed, punching the air. 'Did you hear that, Bosun? She'll try for it! An' you mark my words, Bosun, she'll do us proud! She'll show those other traders' daughters a thing or two!'

5 - By Candlelight

Margareth was almost frantic when Britta at last arrived home, but accepted her sister's apologies with good grace and asked no awkward questions. Maarie would not have been so easily satisfied, but luckily she was still asleep when Britta quietly let herself in by the shop's back door.

'I think Mother will sleep the night through,' said Margareth as Britta sat down to eat the soup her sister had kept warm for her on the stove. 'She was quite peaceful when I looked in on her a few minutes ago. That means she is over the worst of it. She will be up and around tomorrow, I am sure.'

Britta ate her food without tasting it, her mind buzzing with plans. She knew that if she was to compete at the Traders' Hall in the morning, she would have to slip away before her mother and sister woke. There would be a terrible scene if she told them where she was going, and she cringed at the thought of lying outright.

So she yawned often as she washed the dishes, and as soon as they were finished said she would go early to bed.

'I am not surprised,' Margareth said, pulling the kitchen lantern closer to her chair and reaching for her workbasket. 'You must be very tired after your long walk to the harbour and back.'

Britta felt a sharp pang of guilt as she heard the sympathy in the gentle voice. She snatched up a candle, left the room quickly and hurried upstairs.

In the room she shared with Margareth, she made her hasty preparations for the morning, listening every moment for the sound of her mother's voice, or her sister's footstep on the stairs.

Selfish, a voice was saying in her mind, over and over again. *Deceitful. Ungrateful. Reckless.* But her hands did not stop what they were doing for an instant, and her determination did not waver.

When all was done, she threw on her nightdress, put out the candle and climbed into bed. The shadows in the room gathered about her like dark, filmy curtains. She shut her eyes, but her mind was still racing and she knew sleep was very far away.

She took care to lie still and breathe evenly when Margareth crept into the room a little later. She heard her sister get into bed and sigh with relief as she lay down. Again she felt a pang of guilt. Margareth had worked tirelessly all day, without complaint. It was Margareth who deserved sympathy, not her younger sister, who was plotting something that would cause trouble and upset in the house, however it ended.

But that is not my fault, Britta thought fiercely, clenching her fists under the covers. Is there another mother in Del who would object to her daughter trying for the chance to be the Rosalyn Apprentice?

The astounding, troubling events of the day rushed back into her mind. Thoughts of her father, of what her father had done to his family, tormented her, filling her with a bitter mixture of anger and grief.

She glanced at the huddled shape in the bed on the other side of the room. Margareth seemed to have fallen instantly to sleep. No wonder, after the worrying day she had spent. Grimacing, Britta turned over to face the wall and felt for the tattered old book tucked beneath her mattress.

The book had been her secret comfort for years. It was called *A Trader's Life*, and had been written by a man called Sven who had lived long before the Shadowlands invasion. Often Britta read it in the night, when she felt it was safe to do so, but never had she pulled it from its hiding place with such longing as she did now. For now she desperately needed the strength she knew the book could give her … one chapter of it, at least.

Cautiously she lit her candle again, turned to the page she wanted, and began to read:

THE WONDROUS STAFF OF TIER

It was during my second trading voyage, on the ship *Bold Maiden*, that I first saw the mysterious Isle of Tier. It appeared on the horizon at dusk, a misty, shimmering vision of emerald green.

I looked forward to seeing it more closely, and was sorry to find that we were changing course to give it a wide berth. When I asked some members of the crew what the island was, and why we were going out of our way to avoid it, none of them would answer. They merely shook their heads and looked afraid.

I confess I was a little irritated by this, and I waited impatiently for dinner, when at last I was able to question Captain Wrass himself.

He told me a curious story, one of the strangest I ever heard in all my travels. I have heard and read it since, of course, many times. Sometimes the details vary. But Captain Wrass was a great storyteller, and I will never forget the earnest light in his faded blue eyes as he told his tale. I set his version down here, just as I remember it. Readers may make of it what they will …

Once, long ago, a monster called Tier, said to be half man, half turtle, was born to a sorceress who lived on the island of Two Moons in the Silver Sea.

Tier was a gentle soul who wished no one any harm. After his mother went to join her ancestors he stayed on alone in the swamp that was his home. There he lived quietly, moulding amber mud into strange, beautiful shapes that moved, and listening to the music of the birds. But as Tier grew older, larger and stronger in magic, some of his neighbours began to fear him and wish him ill.

They did not dare to kill him, fearing that if they did his ghost would haunt Two Moons forever. So they made another plan.

On the appointed night, a woman Tier trusted lured him from his work. She sang sweetly to him and gave him strong drink made of swamp orchid seeds. When he was deep in a drugged sleep, his enemies bound him with iron chains and dragged him to the shore. They set him adrift on a raft of logs, telling the tide to take him far away from Two Moons.

Tier woke beneath the wide blue vault of the sky, knowing he had been betrayed. He remembered the songs of the woman he had trusted, and cursed her name. He looked at his horny hands, still caked with the living mud of his lost home, and wept for the birdsong he could not longer hear. He struggled to break his chains, but they resisted him. Their iron weakened his magic, as did the salt of the sea.

In his agony, he clenched his fists over the mud that was all he had left of his former life, and cried out piteously for aid. His voice rang like a great bell over the sea and it was heard, though not by human ears.

Great turtles came swimming from far and wide. They gathered around Tier's raft and bore it fast and steadily through the trackless sea. Tier feared he was dreaming the dreams of the dying, but he kept his fists clenched. He never let the mud of his home fall from his hands, and it stayed with him all the while.

After three days and three nights, the turtles steered the raft to land—a black rock so bleak and windswept that it bore not a blade of grass, not a patch of moss. And when Tier felt solid ground beneath him he struggled again and found that over time the salt of the sea had rusted the iron of his chains, so that at last they broke.

He shook off the fragments of the chains and felt magic rush back into his body. The great, humped shell on his back glowed. He stood upright and raised his fists, bellowing to the placid skies. Only the turtles and the seabirds heard him, but what they heard they never forgot.

'This rock has freed me!' the turtle man shouted. 'My own land cast me off, but this rock has taken me in, and it will be rewarded! No longer will it be dead and barren. I will make it fit to be called the Isle of Tier!'

Murmuring magic words, he smeared his mud-caked hands upon the dull black surface of the rock. At once, the rock began to bloom. Ferns sprouted in holes and crevices. Trees hung with fragrant swamp orchids spread over the ragged hills. Water welled up from the central peak and tumbled like a bride's veil down to the sea. And at last the island was a green paradise, ringed by a deadly, hidden reef and the foam-tipped waves of the sea.

It was beautiful—very beautiful. And yet …

'It is not enough,' Tier said. He was remembering his betrayal, and anger was still boiling within him.

He bent and picked up handfuls of the gleaming sand that lay at his feet. He pressed the sand between his mighty hands till it became a Staff—a black diamond Staff into which he poured all his magic, all his grief, all his passion and rage. Then he laboured to a cavern in the island's centre where trees blocked the sun and the air was as dim and fragrant as it had been in the swamp of his birth. He drove the Staff into the island's heart and the island quivered—and lived.

'Behold!' Tier cried. 'From this moment, the Isle of Tier is like no other island in the Silver Sea. From this moment it can move where it wills, and devour other life wherever it finds it. Now it can take revenge on the ordinary mortals who betrayed me. And the Staff that gave it life, the Staff that cures all ills, cannot be taken from me by any man or woman alive.'

So the Hungry Isle was born, and word of it began to spread throughout the Silver Sea. Beautiful and deadly, it prowled its domain like a huge, ravenous beast. Ships, monsters of the deep and even smaller islands that came into its orbit were sucked into its maw and slowly consumed.

Yet in those early years men and women were drawn to it, fascinated by its mysterious beauty and lured by the strong, sweet scent that flowed from it like honey.

Hundreds left their ships at anchor and rowed over the reef to land on the isle's gleaming shore. They came meaning only to spend an hour, but they never left. Becoming enraptured by the magic Staff, they stayed to worship it and fawn on its Master, while the island gorged first on their longboats, and then on their rotting ships.

By the Staff's power these poor wretches lived long in their bondage. But even when their hearts failed at last they remained as wraiths floating in the dim, perfumed air, so wise sailors learned to fear the Hungry Isle, and when it was sighted on the horizon, ships changed course.

The sorcerer Tier survived for centuries, it is said, but life ceased to have flavour for him and there came a time when he was glad to welcome death. He died but the island lived on, a peril to all who sailed the Silver Sea, until one fine day a pirate called Bar-Enoch landed on its shore.

By trickery, Bar-Enoch defied Tier's spell and took the Staff for himself, wresting it from the island's heart and carrying it away to aid him in his wicked career of plunder and bloodshed. So it was that the Isle of Tier could no longer move and feed, and the wraiths were left to haunt its silent forests, ceaselessly cursing Bar-Enoch's name, ceaselessly mourning their loss.

Margareth murmured in her sleep, and Britta froze. But Margareth merely turned over and soon began breathing evenly again. Quietly, Britta turned the page and read the final paragraphs of Sven's story.

As you can imagine, by the time Captain Wrass had finished his tale, I had lost all desire to see the haunted island more closely. Still, my young mind was buzzing with questions. How did the pirate Bar-Enoch thwart the curse of the sorcerer Tier? What happened to him in the end? Where is the magic Staff now?

To this day, I have not discovered the answers to those questions. The one thing that seems certain is that at last Bar-Enoch grew tired of life, as Tier had done, and died. His final resting place is a mystery. But wherever it may be, we may be sure that his dead hand still clutches the wondrous Staff of Tier, which waits for its new master.

Well, Britta thought bitterly, as she had thought so often before, the Staff has its new master now. And what evil has come of it!

The shadows around her bed seemed to sigh and press inward as she closed the book and returned it to its hiding place. She saw that the candle was burning very low, the long, yellow flame wavering deep in a pool of melted wax. Quickly she blew it out, lay back on her pillow and pulled the covers up to her chin.

As she had hoped, the familiar story had made her feel stronger and more determined. She had been caught up in a tragedy that was none of her making. Her father had used his cleverness and talent to find the Staff and take it back to the place of its creation. He had broken faith with all who loved him so that he could have riches beyond his wildest dreams—and live forever.

But his wrongdoing will not ruin my life, too, Britta thought. I will not let it. Father made his choice, and I have the right to make mine.

She closed her eyes and willed herself to sleep. But she dozed only fitfully, and visions of a turtle man with her father's eyes haunted her dreams.

6 - The Harbour

In darkness, after an almost sleepless night, Britta tiptoed from the bedroom, carrying the clothes she had left ready under her bed. She crept down the rickety stairs, mindful of every squeaking tread, and dressed hurriedly in the kitchen behind the shop, scraping her hair into its usual knot at the back of her neck without benefit of mirror or light.

Forcing down a slice of bread and a cup of milk that her stomach kept telling her it did not want, she read the note she planned to leave behind.

> I have gone out and may not be back till late. Will explain everything then. Please do not worry.
>
> Britta

The note seemed even more abrupt than it had when she had penned it, and the last sentence sounded quite ridiculous. Of course her mother and sister would worry if she was away all day without a proper explanation!

For a moment Britta wondered if it would be better not to leave a note at all, then decided that any message was better than none. She propped the scrap of paper against the jug of flowers that stood in the centre of the kitchen table, snatched her cloak from its peg beside the back door and went out into the wet, grey dawn.

She had planned to stop at the bakery to use up some of her extra time. Jantsy started work long before most people in Del were awake, so that the shop racks would be filled with newly baked bread and cakes by opening time. He would give Britta tea, and she would be able to sit in peace in a corner of the warm kitchen while he worked.

That was what she had thought. But when she actually reached the bakery window, and through the blind saw Jantsy's familiar shape moving to and fro between oven and workbench, she suddenly changed her mind and walked on.

The fact was, she felt uneasy about seeing Jantsy this morning. For the first time since she had known him, she felt he disapproved of something she was doing.

Jantsy knew her through and through. They had

been friends since her very first day at Dame Dalmar's little school around the corner from the shop, beside the busy Del pottery. He had been nine, Britta two years younger.

Sometimes Britta still wondered why Jantsy, a confident, popular local boy, had chosen to become the casual protector of a confused and silent new girl whose prim clothes made her the object of curiosity and sometimes teasing in the schoolyard.

She had never asked him about it. She suspected he would not know the answer himself. Whatever the reason, they had been friends ever since.

They did not open their hearts to each other very often. As a rule, they talked of nothing but everyday things. Yet Britta had never wished for another companion. For a very long time now, she had taken it for granted that nothing she could say or do would shock Jantsy, or make him dislike her. Now that comfortable assurance had been shaken.

Hurrying home from the harbour the night before, Jantsy had been strangely silent after she told him Captain Gripp's news. His silence had gone on so long, in fact, that Britta had at last asked him, a little sharply, what the matter was.

Jantsy had said that nothing was the matter—he was just surprised, that was all. And then he had gone quiet again, barely answering as Britta chattered of her plans, and leaving her at the shop door with only a brief murmur of farewell.

No doubt he thinks I will get myself into loads of trouble, Britta thought now, clenching her fists as she trudged on through the fine rain. Well, no doubt I will. I do not need him to remind me of it!

But uneasiness followed her all the way to the harbour. It prevented her lingering along the way or taking shelter anywhere. So she arrived damp, irritable—and ninety minutes early.

Captain Gripp's was the obvious place to wait, but in her present mood Britta felt she could not deal with the fuss that would result if she appeared at the cottage door. She wanted only to be quiet, and could not face the old man's excitement at seeing her, his bellowed orders to Bosun, and the barrage of well-meaning advice that would surely follow. Cursing the weather, she looked around for somewhere else to pass the time.

The door of the handsome new Traders' Hall was shut. Perhaps there were people inside, but Britta had no intention of knocking. Her early arrival might be reported, and it never did for a trader to appear too eager.

So she strode past the hall without a glance and headed instead to something that lay beyond it—a little shelter beside the sea wall at the far end of the harbour graveyard.

The shelter was a simple affair—just a flat roof supported by four stone pillars. It was barely visible through the rain, but passing by on brighter days

Britta had noticed that a sturdy wooden table and two long benches stood beneath it. No doubt the shelter had been intended as a place for mourners to rest, a quiet place where they could sit a while and look out at the sea to soothe their grief. For Britta, it would be a welcome refuge from the rain.

She had never felt the slightest desire to visit the graveyard on her way to see Captain Gripp. But as she trudged towards the shelter over the thick mat of sea daisies that grew between the rows of graves, she could not help glancing at the stones she passed.

Some were true gravestones. Others were simply tablets placed in memory of souls lost or buried at sea.

In memory of Josh, beloved son of Lalla and Vin, taken in his 24th year while defending the Golden Dragon *from sea serpent attack … Trader 'Spark' Bono, 42 years, lost to fever at Isthmus … Here lies Zandalin, gallant Resistance fighter, Del Harbour Master for 15 years … Beneath this stone sleeps Mikah, 45 years, first Captain of the* Star of Deltora …

Mikah … first Captain of the Star of Deltora … Britta stopped, staring at the gravestone. Suddenly she felt chilled to the bone. Suddenly she understood her mother's shuddering terror of the harbour, her mother's determination to hide away from it, never to see it again.

She forced herself to read the carved words—all of them.

Beneath this
stone lies

MIKAH

45 years, first Captain of
the Star of Deltora.

Foully betrayed by one
he trusted, he perished
attempting to bring his
ship home. His courage
will never be forgotten.

Foully betrayed by one he trusted …

Shivering, Britta turned from the grave and walked quickly on through the misty rain, wrapping her cloak more tightly around her chest.

I knew all this before, she told herself. Seeing that grave should make no difference to me.

But the terrible words chipped in stone were still dancing before her eyes as she reached the graveyard's end. Perhaps this was why, when she saw a long, bizarre figure laid out like a corpse on one of the benches of the shelter, she started and cried out.

There was a blur of movement and the next moment the figure was no longer lying down but on its feet, towering over Britta with a deadly-looking spear in its hand.

Britta jumped back, instinctively holding up her own hands to show they were empty of weapons. The towering figure blinked. The spear was lowered, then tucked back into a long leather pouch slung over the stranger's shoulder.

'Ha! What a fright you gave me!' the stranger exclaimed, laughing. And Britta, her heart hammering in her chest, was astonished to hear by the voice that her companion was not a man, as she had supposed, but a woman—and a young woman at that.

Yet never had she seen a woman so tall, so broad-shouldered and wearing such man-like clothes! Never had she seen a woman whose idea of jewellery was a wide band of beaten metal clasped around one arm and matching earrings as big as jam jar lids. And never, even at the harbour where so many foreign sailors roamed the streets, had she seen a woman whose head was shaved, and whose bare, brown scalp was marked with patterns of swirling red.

'It is the tradition where I come from,' the bald stranger said, patting her decorated skull. And Britta felt her face grow hot as she realised that she had been staring in a way her mother would have called very ill bred.

The stranger burst out laughing again. 'Never mind!' she cried. 'You look just as odd to me, I assure you, huddled out there like a poor, bedraggled little nodnap! Come in out of the rain, for pity's sake!'

Britta felt a prickle of irritation. 'You are the

one who aimed a spear at me and drove me out!' she snapped, stepping smartly back under shelter. 'And what is a nodnap, anyway?'

'A bird,' said the stranger. 'Thousands of them live on the Painted Plain near Broome, where I live. They make very good eating.'

Broome. Britta frowned, remembering lessons from school. Broome was a coastal town in Deltora's south-east, in the territory of the ruby. Dame Dalmar, looking down her nose, had told the class that the people of Broome were very loud, wild and vulgar. That was hardly surprising, because they were all descended from castaways, pirates and mutineers.

Benn, a plump, clever boy who Dame Dalmar often found impertinent, had put up his hand. Del's captain of the guard, Benn had said, was married to a woman of Broome. And the captain of the guard was highly respected, having helped the king and queen of Deltora to end the Shadowlands invasion.

Scarlet with irritation, Dame Dalmar had snapped that strange bonds were often formed in times of war. After many years of peace, however, things were naturally quite different. She would not dream of questioning the choice of the captain of the guard, but she herself would not care to know a person with no idea of proper manners.

Glancing sideways at her companion, who had sat down and begun trimming her fingernails with a huge knife she had taken from her belt, Britta decided that Dame Dalmar had been perfectly right. Very straight-backed, she moved to the bench on the other side of the table and smoothed her damp hair, trying to tuck straggling locks back into the knot at the nape of her neck.

'My name is Jewel,' the young woman of Broome said, without looking up. 'What is yours?'

'Britta.' And because, somehow, the single word seemed too abrupt, Britta added politely: 'And what are you doing in Del harbour, Jewel? Are you seeking work on a trading ship?'

'In a way,' said Jewel, with an edge to her voice. 'I am hoping to sail on the *Star of Deltora*.'

She did not raise her eyes as Britta jumped, but she must have sensed her companion's shock, because she smiled as she continued working on her nails.

'Oh, yes,' she said softly. 'Despite all appearances, little nodnap, I am a candidate in the Rosalyn Trust competition. I aim to become Mab's Apprentice—as, I suppose, do you!'

Britta bit back the confused apology that sprang to her lips. How could she apologise for being a thoughtless snob?

Jewel grinned. 'And now, if you will excuse me, I will continue my nap. I walked a long way last night, and have had little sleep.'

She put away her knife and stretched out on the bench again.

After that, the only sounds were the dripping

of the rain rolling from the shelter roof, the lapping of the sluggish waves against the sea wall and the desolate cries of seabirds. Britta wriggled her toes in her wet boots, flapped the edges of her clammy cloak, and wished the sun would come out. She heard the harbour clock strike seven and all at once realised how tired she felt. She, too, had had very little sleep.

Jewel was breathing as evenly and peacefully as if her hard bench were a feather bed. Plainly she was used to sleeping anywhere she could, and was quite untroubled by the idea of lying down in a public place.

Britta tried to feel scornful but discovered that her main emotion was envy. Still, she knew there was no way she could follow Jewel's example. The imagined horror of her mother at the very thought of her sleeping outdoors was too strong. She bent over the tabletop, pillowing her cheek on her folded arms.

Just for a few minutes, she thought, letting her eyes close. Just to stop my eyelids feeling so heavy. If I hear anyone coming I can sit back up in an instant …

The next thing she knew, someone was shaking her shoulder.

'For pity's sake, will the girl never wake?' a voice roared somewhere above her head. 'Stir yourself, little nodnap! We must go!'

7 - Rivals

Britta sat bolt upright, and for an instant did not know where she was. Then she saw the rough wooden table, the pillars of the shelter and watery sunlight. She saw Jewel of Broome with her hands on her hips, scowling and shaking her painted head. And she heard the harbour clock beginning to chime the hour.

'It is eight o'clock!' cried Jewel. 'They are going in! Make haste!'

She turned and set off through the graveyard with an easy, loping stride. Jumping up, blinking and confused, Britta felt a stab of annoyance. Why had Jewel not waited for her?

Then it struck her that Jewel owed her nothing—it was the other way around. She and Jewel were rivals, yet Jewel had stayed to wake her. A less generous person might have crept away leaving her sleeping companion to miss the test entirely!

Britta squeezed out from behind the table and began to run, slipping and sliding on the wet daisies, frantically tucking in the flapping tail of her shirt. The clock had stopped chiming. Over the gravestones she could see young women filing through the door of the Traders' Hall while a portly woman marked their names off on a list. Already Jewel had joined the end of the line, which was shortening rapidly.

By the time Britta arrived at the Hall, breathless, all the other candidates were inside. The portly woman had put away her list and was preparing to follow.

'Wait!' Britta gasped. 'Please—'

The woman half-turned, frowning. She looked Britta up and down, plainly not liking what she saw.

'I am a candidate!' Britta panted. 'Britta! Britta of—of Del.'

Taking her time, the woman drew out her list and consulted it. The rumbling sound of someone making a speech drifted through the doorway and Britta jiggled with impatience.

'Ah yes,' the woman said, tapping the blank space beside Britta's name with one stubby finger. 'Well, my girl, it was clearly stated on the entry form that testing would begin at eight o'clock precisely. All the other candidates were punctual and are already in the assembly room. I fear you are too late.'

A smug little smile trembled on her lips. Plainly she was enjoying this chance to show her authority.

If Britta had not been so flurried, she would no doubt have kept her temper. She would have used flattery to get her way, as she had done so often when dealing with a difficult customer in the shop. She would have apologised humbly for her lateness, and pleaded to be allowed to enter the Traders' Hall despite her fault. She might even have pretended to shed tears. Then the woman at the door, her vanity satisfied, would have graciously agreed to let her in, and many things afterwards would have been different.

But Britta *was* flurried, and the little wave of girlish laughter that drifted through the door at that moment raised her impatience to fever pitch.

'I am not too late,' she snapped as the rumbling voice began speaking again. 'The testing has not begun yet—we can both hear that plainly. Please let me pass.'

The woman in the doorway seemed to swell. Her face darkened with anger. Then, as another gale of laughter made it clear that Britta was perfectly right, she pursed her lips and abruptly stood aside.

Bolting past her, Britta found herself in a spacious entry room. Jewel's pouch of spears and an array of cloaks hung from hooks fastened to one of the walls. The voice she had heard from outside was booming through an open doorway to her right.

She listened as she hung her cloak with the others and tiptoed to the doorway, nervously smoothing back the wisps of hair that clung to her hot cheeks.

'During her voyage, which is expected to take no longer than twelve weeks, the *Star of Deltora* will call at three ports,' the booming voice said. 'At the first of these ports, each of the three finalists will be given ten gold coins with which to buy trading goods.'

Ten gold coins! Britta thought dazedly. She had never seen so much money together in one place in her whole life.

On a small table by the door lay a box of pins and one lonely white card threaded with red ribbon and bearing the words 'Britta of Del'. Hoping she was doing the right thing, Britta hastily pinned the card to her shirt. She could feel the portly woman's eyes boring into her back, but resisted the impulse to look round.

'Further trading may be done at the second and third ports, but no further funds will be made available,' the voice went on. 'In a nutshell, those are the basic terms of the Rosalyn Trust. May I wish you all good luck—and may the best candidates win!'

There was a burst of applause. Gritting her teeth, Britta slipped through the doorway.

At the front of the long assembly room, about thirty young women were sitting in chairs arranged in rows before a raised platform. All were clapping vigorously. Many of them wore the crisp, high-necked shirts, smart little jackets and plain skirts that were regarded as proper for Del traders' daughters. Most of the others, like Britta herself, wore a less expensive version of the same thing. Only a few, like Jewel, who was sprawled in a chair at the end of the back row, were dressed differently.

On the platform stood a silver-haired man with pouchy cheeks and a small white moustache that curled up at the ends. He smiled, waiting for the applause to end. Beside him sat a bone-thin old woman. Her hair was bright red and twisted high on her head so it looked like the crest of an exotic bird. Her hooded eyes, their lids painted sky blue, raked the clapping candidates, resting first on one face, then on another.

Mab, thought Britta.

She had never seen the legendary Trader Rosalyn before, but she knew she had made no mistake. In the old, safe days when Dare Larsett had been a Rosalyn fleet trader, Britta's mother had often talked scathingly of Mab's dyed hair and painted face, and of the gold hoops that hung from Mab's earlobes.

It was whispered that Mab wore trousers when she was at sea, but today she was respectably if gaudily dressed in a rich blue skirt and a tight-fitting jacket with a high collar and many brass buttons.

Seeing an empty seat near the end of a row, Britta walked quickly towards it, thankful that the applause covered the sound of her footsteps. Murmuring apologies, she squeezed past two impeccably dressed candidates who looked so alike that they might have been sisters, and tried to ignore their stares as she sank into the vacant chair.

She understood why the seat had been left free when she saw her right-hand neighbour. The two tidy young ladies at the end of the row had preferred not to sit beside someone who looked more like a sailor from a foreign port than a Del trader.

The girl was tall and rangy. She was wearing a faded, roughly woven tunic over loose trousers that were tucked into high, mud-stained boots, and a patterned scarf was knotted carelessly at her throat. Her lustrous brown hair hung almost to her waist. Some, at the front, had been plaited into thin braids that jingled with tiny ornaments tied on with strips of leather. Like the other candidates, she was clapping, but in a slow, lazy way that seemed almost insolent. According to her name card, which was casually tied to her belt instead of pinned tidily on her tunic, her name was Sky of Rithmere.

Britta knew little of Rithmere except that it was an inland town far to Del's north-west, set on the great River Broad. She seemed to remember that trade thrived there, but she would not have expected anyone brought up so far from the sea to enter the Rosalyn contest.

As if sensing Britta's curious stare, Sky looked round. Britta caught a brief glimpse of a lean, olive-skinned face with strong, slanting brows and calculating black eyes. Then the corner of the girl's wide mouth twitched and she turned to face the front again. Plainly she had summed up Britta at a glance and had dismissed her as serious competition.

Very ruffled, Britta looked up at the platform, and with a little shock saw that Mab was watching her. Plainly her late arrival had been noted. She forced her hands to remain still, though the urge to smooth her untidy hair again was almost irresistible.

There was no spark of recognition in Mab's hooded eyes. How could there be? Mab had doted on Dare Larsett. He had been her protégé and pet—the son, some said, that she had never had—but his family had never been of any interest to her. Mab preferred to forget, Britta had once heard Maarie complain, that Larsett even *had* a family. Mab liked to think he was hers alone, and that the life he led with her on the sea and in foreign ports was his only life.

Well, she paid for her jealousy, Britta thought. She was betrayed and abandoned in the end, just as Mother, Margareth and I were. And now it suits me that she shunned us. If someone recognises me, it will not be Mab, at least.

She returned the old trader's hard stare calmly, managing not to blink or look down, but it was a huge relief when the applause ended at last and Mab turned to face the silver-haired man again.

'Are there any questions?' the man asked, looking around pleasantly.

Britta had a hundred questions, but for all she knew they had been answered before she arrived, so she did not dare to put up her hand.

A chair scraped the floor. The man nodded in the direction of the sound, which had been somewhere behind Britta.

'Can you tell us the names of the three ports the *Star of Deltora* will be visiting, Trader Sorrel?'

Britta recognised the rich, confident voice at once. The questioner was Jewel. She could well imagine the tall young woman of Broome standing up in the back row, her painted head gleaming under the lights.

A chorus of smothered giggles echoed around the room, as if most of the candidates knew the question was foolish. The silver-haired man smiled.

'No, Candidate,' he said, shaking his head. 'The rules of the Trust state that to ensure fair play the finalists will be told the ports of call only when their ship has left Del harbour.'

So the idea is that all finalists begin with an equal chance, is it? Britta thought wryly. But Mab and her people must know that the traders' daughters here have certainly already been coached on what to do in every possible port!

She saw Sky's jaw tighten, and was grimly pleased. At least the odious Rithmere girl was as badly off as she was, and knew it! It almost made up for the fact that the two young women on her other side were looking extremely smug.

There were no more questions, and in moments all the candidates were rising to their feet while Mab and Trader Sorrel left the platform in stately fashion and disappeared through a side door.

People around Britta began picking up their chairs and moving towards the back of the assembly room, where rows of tables stood. Blindly she copied them, cursing herself for having missed the first part of Trader Sorrel's speech. She had no idea what she was supposed to do.

'Choose a table and sit down, but on no account turn over the test paper,' Jewel's voice muttered in her ear. 'You are out straight away if you do.'

Britta looked round, but already Jewel was striding away, her chair swinging lightly in one hand.

The stout woman who had tried to stop Britta at the Traders' Hall door was standing at the front of the rows of tables, watching the candidates closely. Her face and neck were still mottled with angry red patches, and when she caught sight of Britta her eyes narrowed unpleasantly.

Knowing that the woman was watching her every move, Britta found an empty table in the dimmest corner of the room. Shakily she pushed her chair into place and sat down, noting the blank yellow back of the booklet in front of her. She felt sick. If Jewel had not warned her she might easily have picked up the test paper, not knowing it was forbidden. Folding her hands tightly in her lap to show that she was not going to make that mistake, she looked up, and felt even sicker as she surprised a flash of disappointment in the watching woman's eyes.

The woman cleared her throat fussily. 'I will be supervising your test today, Candidates,' she said, without a glimmer of a smile. 'For those of you who do not know, I am the Senior Managing Officer of the Rosalyn Trust. My name is Zoolah.'

Zoolah! Britta caught her breath. Captain Gripp had mentioned that name briefly the night before, while he was saying goodbye. Suddenly awkward, as if he was forcing himself to mention something distasteful, he had said that Britta was certain to meet a woman called Zoolah at the Traders' Hall. He had warned Britta not to offend Zoolah, because she was famous for holding a grudge.

Well, it is too late to worry about that now, Britta thought ruefully, and cursed herself for not being more cautious.

'Your test papers are in front of you,' Zoolah said, her back straight as a ruler and her chest puffed up with importance. 'You may now print your name and the name of your sponsor clearly on the back of your test, but do not turn it over.'

She waited, watching beadily to see that her charges, and particularly Britta, did as they were told and no more. Then she cleared her throat again.

'You have ninety minutes to complete the paper,' she said, pointing to a large clock on the wall. 'You may begin … now!'

8 - The Test

There was a rustle as every candidate turned her paper over. Britta stared at the first question. It was a fairly simple mathematical problem. No one who had worked in a shop as she had, taking money and giving change all day, would have had trouble working it out. Britta wrote in the answer and moved to the next question. It was a similar problem—a little trickier than the first, but nothing she could not handle.

After ten mathematical problems, there were questions about words. Again, the first were easy and the later ones more difficult, but Britta felt confident of her answers.

She worked rapidly through the first page of the booklet, her spirits rising. If the whole test was like this, she was certain to do well!

Then she turned the page, and her confidence

was jolted. The questions here were of quite another kind.

> **Q ~ If a trader buys a cargo of cooking oil cheaply, what will make the oil costly to her after all?**

There were a few possible answers to that. If the trader's ship sank, for example, the oil would be lost. But Britta did not think the examiners were considering disasters. She remembered the many jars of pickled onions cluttering the shelves in her mother's shop, and wrote:

> If the trader cannot sell the cheap oil because no one wishes to buy it, the money spent on it, however little, will have been wasted.
> The money spent on the trading voyage will have been wasted also.
> Therefore the oil purchase has been a costly mistake.

And so it went on, each question a little harder to answer than the one before. Britta read, thought, wrote, and by the middle of the second page she suddenly found that she was enjoying herself immensely. She had never enjoyed tests at school—but these problems were so interesting!

The other candidates were scribbling all around her. Now and then someone would sigh or a page would turn. Zoolah sat silently at the front, watching. Britta moved on to the third page, then the fourth, then the fifth and last. There were only two questions on the fifth page. She looked eagerly at the top one:

> **Q ~ What is a good trader's most important quality? (circle one)**
>
> **Knowledge**
> **Confidence**
> **Honesty**
> **Determination**
> **Understanding of people**
> **Mathematical ability**
> **Outgoing personality**
> **Experience**

Britta's pencil hovered over the paper. All the qualities seemed important to her. She could not decide between them. She jumped as Zoolah's voice cut through her thoughts.

'You have five minutes more, Candidates.'

Britta quickly circled 'Understanding of people'. After all, that was what had helped her to sell a whole cheese yesterday. Still …

Stifling her doubts, she hurried on to the next question. When she read it, she felt her face grow hot.

Q ~ Why do you wish to be the
Trader Rosalyn Apprentice?

Why? Britta thought, her cheeks burning. Because trading is in my blood. Because I lost my birthright through no fault of my own. Because the *Star of Deltora* once belonged to my family and this is my only chance to get her back.

She could write none of this, of course, for fear of revealing who she was. And to write down the other things that sprang to mind—that she was stifled at home, that she longed to sail the wide seas and see new, interesting people and places, would impress no one.

She sat motionless, her pencil gripped in her fingers, while all around her the other candidates wrote furiously. This last question was surely the most important one of all. Time was ticking away. And here she sat, paralysed, unable to write a word.

In her panic, Britta found her mind veering away from the question in front of her and focusing on the previous one. Had she chosen the wrong quality? Mab and the other traders were old. No doubt they thought that knowledge and experience were vital. Britta had so little of either that she had not considered marking one of them.

Something clicked in her brain. She looked back at the last question, holding her breath, and rapidly scrawled the answer that had come to her:

73

I have always wanted to be a
trader and I think I could be a
good one with the right teaching.
I am confident, determined and as
honest as possible. I have an outgoing
personality, good mathematical ability,
and some understanding of people.
But I have very little knowledge or
experience and I know that to be
a good trader I need both. As the
Trader Rosalyn Apprentice I would
be taught by the best, and would
gain experience that I could not hope
to gain any other way.

'Pencils down!' shrilled Zoolah. 'Remain seated while I collect your papers.'

Britta let her pencil fall and flexed her cramped fingers. Gazing at what she had just written, it suddenly struck her that the first part sounded conceited. She had not considered that when she had seized on the idea of using the qualities listed in the question before to frame her answer.

With a sinking feeling she handed over her test as Zoolah reached her table. I wrote nothing but the truth, she told herself. I even put 'as honest as possible' instead of just 'honest'.

But that, perhaps, had been a mistake. Britta looked around at her fellow candidates under her eyelashes. Would any of them have told the truth about something like that? Jewel might have, perhaps. But none of the traders' daughters would have dreamed of it, and Sky of Rithmere would have laughed at the very idea.

Zoolah bustled out, the papers tucked under her arm, and a few minutes later Trader Sorrel returned.

'Now, Candidates, I will escort you to the traders' luncheon room, where refreshments will be served,' he said breezily. 'I am sure that after your efforts of the past hour and a half you are all ready for a rest.'

Dutiful giggles followed his announcement. But as everyone rose and trooped out of the assembly room, Britta saw that even the neatest, glossiest candidate looked a little the worse for wear. She was not the only one, it seemed, who had found the test a challenge.

Slightly comforted, she shuffled along with the chattering crowd as Sorrel led the way through a door at the far side of the entry room. Beyond the door was a broad hallway lined with paintings of ships, framed documents and displays of objects that were part of Del's trading history.

'What did you say was the most important quality in a good trader, Sisely?' Britta heard the smartly dressed girl in front of her ask. 'I chose "Confidence", because Father always says—'

'I circled "Determination",' the girl's companion whispered back. 'But I am sure it was wrong. Oh, and some of those word questions were very hard, Lenah!

Is "curr*ant*" the pull of the tide, and "curr*ent*" the dried fruit? Or is it the other way round?'

As the girl called Lenah shrugged helplessly, the fair-haired candidate in front of them glanced over her shoulder. Her pretty, heart-shaped face, with its large, slightly slanted blue eyes and small rosebud mouth, made Britta think of a kitten—a kitten who had never failed to secure all the cream she wanted.

'The dried fruit ends in "ant", Sisely,' the kitten girl said with a pitying smile. 'It is easy to remember—you just have to think that *ants* like *currants,* but don't like water.' Still smiling, she turned back to face the front, saw an opening in the crowd and slid gracefully through it till she was just behind Trader Sorrel.

'Trust Vashti to know,' Lenah muttered. 'No doubt she got everything right.'

'Yes.' Sisely sighed, as they came to a halt while people at the front of the crowd began filtering into the luncheon room. 'I really cannot think why the rest of us even bothered to come. Vashti will be named Apprentice in the end—everyone knows that! I *told* Mother, but she *insisted*—'

'There are *three* finalists, remember,' her friend broke in. 'Vashti will be one of them, of course, but who knows what might happen on the trial voyage? She might fall overboard and drown—or even worse! After all, life can be very dangerous at sea.' Mischievously she jerked her head at a framed letter on the wall beside her.

'Hush, Lenah!' Sisely hissed, spluttering with laughter. 'Oh, Lenah, you are *terrible!*'

Britta looked curiously at the letter. It was smudged with something that looked like blood. As she read the first line, her stomach turned over.

I am Mikah, Captain of the Star of Deltora. The ship's Log is at the bottom of the sea. I write this message so that my story will not die with me.

Four days ago Dare Larsett found the magic Staff of Tier & made himself its Master. He struck me down & took charge of the ship, guiding it to the haunted isle where the Staff was made & where it will be most powerful.

When the wraiths of the island came across the water to meet him, chanting his name, the crew mutinied. Poor wretches, I do not blame them. Larsett raised the Staff & killed them all. Then he took the landing boat to shore. To my shame, I lay still, pretending to be dead. I knew I could not stop him.

My wounds are grave. My strength is failing. I will try to steer the Star home, for as long as I am able.

To my loving sister, I leave my worldly goods. I send my grateful respects to Mab, the Trader Rosalyn, who paid for my care & continued to employ me after my left hand was taken by a serpent, long ago. I cannot say how bitterly I now regret leaving her service to sail with Dare Larsett.

For over half her life, Britta had heard people speaking of this grim, hasty message. Nothing in it was new to her. But knowing the story of her father's guilt was one thing—seeing the message itself, penned by Mikah's own hand, was different. Like the tombstone in the graveyard, it was too real to ignore. Suddenly she could hardly breathe.

Smothering their giggles, Lenah and Sisely moved on. The crowd behind Britta pressed forward, forcing her to follow, but just inside the luncheon room doorway she stopped, shrinking to one side and flattening herself against the wall.

Young women streamed past her, making for a table where tea, cakes and bowls of fruit had been set out. She returned their curious glances coldly, but inside she was fighting for control.

I cannot go through with this, she thought wildly. Sooner or later I will be found out. Someone who saw me as a child will recognise me! Someone will remember that Dare Larsett's second daughter was called 'Britta'! Oh, why did I listen to Captain Gripp? It was madness—madness—to think I could get away with it!

Her eyes blurred. The room seemed to be filled with swirling shadows. Suddenly all she wanted to do was turn and run—to scuttle home and hide. But candidates were still crowding through the door. She would have to wait till she could slip away unnoticed.

Jewel was one of the last to come in. She gave Britta a friendly look, and receiving only a frozen stare in response, shrugged and strolled on.

Soon the tea table was thronged with young women. Their chatter rose till it sounded to Britta like the excited squabbling of a flock of birds.

Now, Britta thought. Now, while no one is watching me. She turned to escape through the doorway, and almost collided with someone sauntering in.

It was the girl with the dangling, rattling braids— Sky of Rithmere. She grabbed Britta's shoulders to steady herself, then raised a scornful eyebrow as Britta tore away from her with a gasp of shock.

'Are you afraid you will catch something from me, trader's daughter?' Sky drawled, her low, husky voice filled with grim amusement. 'Well, never mind! It seems you will have something else to think about before long.'

Britta had no idea what she meant. All she could think about was that as soon as the doorway was clear, she could leave. But Sky did not budge. She stood perfectly still, a mocking smile on her lips, staring not at Britta but at something behind Britta's left shoulder.

Britta's skin prickled. At the same moment, she realised that the chatter in the room had died and complete silence had fallen.

Slowly she turned. There stood Trader Sorrel, looking very serious, and the woman Zoolah, whose nostrils were pinched as if she could smell something unpleasant.

'Britta?' Sorrel murmured. 'Mab wishes to speak to you. Please come this way.'

9 - The Announcement

So there was to be no escape. In dread, Britta allowed herself to be ushered into the silence of a corridor lined with doors, and then into what Trader Sorrel called 'the conference room'. There, at the far end of a long, polished table that almost filled the room, sat Mab, her elbows propped on a pile of test papers, her hands clasped under her beaky nose.

Sorrel told Britta to sit at the other end of the table. He and Zoolah took the chairs on Mab's right and left.

Mab leaned forward a little and began to speak. With her crest of bright hair and painted eyelids she looked so like a sailor's parrot that Britta had assumed her voice would be harsh. Instead, it was low and musical.

'Before we begin, Candidate, please be aware that this interview does not mean you will necessarily be one of the chosen finalists,' Mab said. 'The test papers are still to be properly marked, but to save time I will be seeing every girl whose answers to the last two questions showed promise.'

And so startled, so dazed with relief was Britta to realise that she was not discovered, not recognised, not about to be ejected from the Traders' Hall in disgrace, that almost everything after that was a blur.

Mab asked questions and somehow Britta replied. Sorrel listened, smoothing his moustache with one finger. Zoolah made an occasional note on a pad of paper in front of her. The only moment that Britta could clearly recall afterwards came right at the end.

Mab suddenly asked her to describe the best bargain she had ever made.

Britta was taken by surprise, and instead of talking about the whole cheese or something equally sensible, she found herself blurting out the truth. She spoke of trading, at the age of ten, her only pair of warm gloves for the book that had become her most treasured possession.

'It was on the tray of a street peddler, and was not in good condition even then,' she heard herself saying. 'Its name is *A Trader's Life*, and it was written long ago by a Del trader called Sven.'

The moment the words left her lips, she knew she had made a blunder.

Zoolah sniffed, Mab looked grim and Sorrel's half smile became a little fixed. Plainly they were not impressed, but Britta knew it was too late to take her words back so she ploughed on, trying to make the best of it. She admitted that she had not thought the book was particularly valuable. She had not traded for it because she thought she could sell it at a better price. She had wanted it for herself—wanted it badly.

She did not say, of course, that she had smuggled *A Trader's Life* home and kept it hidden ever since, because her mother would have thrown it into the stove if she had found it. She did not admit that she had pretended to have lost her gloves, and borne Maarie's scolding in guilty silence. Remembering that she was supposed to be an orphan, she merely said that she still had the book, and had never regretted the bargain.

'*A Trader's Life* is very out of date, and it is filled with fanciful tales,' Zoolah remarked, not troubling to conceal her scorn. 'You would have done better to borrow a more respectable text from Captain Gripp if you could not afford to buy one.'

Britta felt herself blushing. 'I have read more modern books since. But at the time, Trader Sven's book was a great comfort to me. It kept alive my hopes of being a trader myself one day.' She could have said much more, but she pressed her lips together and did not.

For how could she admit that when she was ten she had not yet found her way back to Captain Gripp? How could she explain how desolate she had felt, exiled from the harbour, marooned in the city's centre? How could she tell of the far better copy of *A Trader's Life* that had been in her father's library, before she was old enough to read it and before the library had been sold along with everything else? And how could she say that seeing that dog-eared book on the peddler's tray had been for her like discovering water in a desert?

Mab dismissed her very soon after that, and Sorrel and Zoolah led her back to the luncheon room. The other candidates stared as she came in.

'Take some refreshment, Britta,' Sorrel said, with a slight bow. 'You have nothing to do now but wait.'

'Thank you,' Britta managed to say. To her own ears, her voice sounded as feeble as the squeak of a mouse.

Sorrel leaned forward. 'You did very well, on the whole,' he murmured. 'Very well.'

Then he and his companion were gone.

Britta turned to the untidy tea table. She could not have eaten anything to save her life, but suddenly she was so thirsty she could have seized one of the great silver teapots and drunk from the spout.

She poured herself some lukewarm tea and gulped it down. No one approached her. In that crowded room she stood quite alone, in a little island of space. Out of the corner of her eye she saw Sorrel and Zoolah ushering the fair, confident candidate Vashti from the room.

Vashti will be named Apprentice in the end—everyone knows that!

The words echoed dismally in Britta's mind. She poured herself more tea, drank it, and took a few deep breaths. Only then did she see Jewel standing not far away, loading a plate with a fresh helping of honey cakes and sweetplums. It was a relief to see a familiar face.

'Hello, Jewel,' Britta ventured.

It would not have surprised her if the woman of Broome had ignored her, but Jewel turned and nodded, though without a smile.

'So—you were granted an interview, little nodnap,' she said. 'How did you fare?'

Britta sighed. 'Not very well, I fear. I am sure that Vashti—that candidate who has just been taken out—will do far better.'

'No doubt she will,' Jewel said cheerfully. 'From what I have heard since I have been in here, Vashti's father has been training her and her younger sisters for years with this contest in mind. He already has three ships of his own, but he wants control of the Trader Rosalyn fleet as well—especially the *Star of Deltora*.'

Seeing Britta wince, she shrugged and bit into a sweetplum. Purple juice ran down her chin and she wiped it away with the back of her hand. 'I reason that Mab must know this as well as everyone else does, and will make allowances,' she added with her mouth full. 'Mab is no fool, by all accounts.'

She regarded Britta with her head on one side. 'You are as pale as a jellyfish. A little better than when I saw you beside the door, but not much. You are probably hungry. Have a honey cake! They are very good.'

Britta's stomach heaved and she shook her head.

Jewel laughed, but not unkindly. 'Then take some for me. I cannot fit any more onto this plate, and free food is never to be sneezed at. It is a long way back to Broome.'

'You may not be going back,' Britta said, trying to sound breezy. 'For all you know, you will be sailing on the *Star of Deltora* tomorrow.'

Jewel shook her head, her huge earrings swinging. 'I fear I have no hope of an interview, however I did in the test. I should not have asked that question about the ports. It made me look stupid.'

'It did not!' Britta exclaimed. 'It was a very sensible question—for anyone who is not a Del trader's daughter!'

She heaped a plate with cakes and she and Jewel walked together to some chairs grouped around a low table in one corner of the room. Two of the chairs were occupied, but the young women sitting there jumped up and edged away as soon as Jewel appeared.

'Stay with me and you will always find a seat!' Jewel chortled. But Britta could see that she was not as careless of the insult as she pretended.

They sat in silence, watching the eddying crowd. Most of the candidates were eating, drinking and chatting, trying hard to seem at ease. Britta looked for Sky of Rithmere, and caught sight of her leaning against the wall on the other side of the room, looking rather bored and playing absently with one of the little ornaments she wore tied to her braids. After about half an hour Vashti came back, looking more like a satisfied kitten than ever, and Sorrel and Zoolah approached another trader's daughter and led her away.

Time crawled by. At lunchtime fresh tea was brought out, together with platters of sandwiches, grilled vegetables and spiced rice patties. Britta went for tea but collected some food as well. Her stomach had stopped churning and at last she felt able to eat.

Sorrel and Zoolah came and went, came and went, collecting candidates and returning them. After a while Britta stopped trying to count the interviews, or see who was being summoned.

As the afternoon wore on, the tension in the room increased. Chatter had become subdued, and a few of the candidates—some of those who had not yet been granted an interview, Britta guessed—looked near to tears. She mentioned this to Jewel, who by now was stretched out in her chair, half asleep.

Jewel nodded. 'I heard someone say that the finalists would be announced by five-thirty at the latest,' she said without opening her eyes. 'That means the interviews must end soon. Judging by the squeaks of the door, there have been twelve already, counting yours. I would not be surprised if the thirteenth is the lucky last.'

And at that moment, Britta saw Sorrel and Zoolah moving towards them.

'Jewel!' she whispered impulsively. 'One of the things Mab might ask is what your best bargain has been! Think about it!'

'What?' Jewel's eyes opened. 'Why should …?' The words died in her throat as she saw Sorrel and Zoolah standing before her.

'Jewel of Broome?' Trader Sorrel murmured. 'Mab wishes to speak to you. Please come this way.'

For once stunned into silence, Jewel stood up and went with them.

In a little less than the usual half hour, she was back. The crowd parted for her as she strode across the room.

'By the stars, I would rather fight a sea serpent barehanded than do that again,' she muttered when she reached Britta. 'But I must thank you. Mab *did* ask me about my best bargain, right at the end. I could well have been flummoxed and made a stupid answer if you had not warned me.'

'There is no need for thanks,' Britta replied stiffly, fighting down the bitter memory of her own answer. 'I owed you a favour—two favours, in fact.'

Jewel laughed. 'Consider the debt paid in full. And by the way, I was right about one thing, at least.

They said my interview was the last.'

Over the next hour, the crowd thinned as most of the candidates who had not been interviewed left the room, some downcast, some resentful, and others swaggering, pretending not to care. The young women who remained talked less and less. Everyone was watching the door to the conference room corridor.

Britta sprang nervously to her feet as at last the door opened and the silver-haired figure of Trader Sorrel appeared. Sorrel shut the door behind him, took two steps forward and smoothed his moustache.

'Thank you for your patience, Candidates,' he said in his deep voice. 'It has been hard to choose finalists from such a fine group of young women ...'

Get on with it! Britta thought, and knew by the anxious faces she saw around her that every other candidate in the room was sharing her feelings.

Finishing his graceful introduction at last, Sorrel regarded his restless audience benignly.

'I will keep you waiting no longer,' he said. 'I ask each finalist to join me here as her name is called.' He glanced at a small card in his hand and raised his voice slightly. 'Vashti, daughter of Irma and Loy of Del!'

Amid a spatter of dutiful applause, the kitten girl moved forward. Sorrel shook her hand. She moved to stand beside him, flushed and smiling but quite composed, not a hair out of place.

Sorrel cleared his throat and glanced at the card again. 'Sky of Rithmere!'

There was a moment's confused silence, then a chorus of gasps as Sky sauntered out of the crowd, the ornaments on her braids rattling softly.

Sorrel greeted her with the same courtesy as he had greeted Vashti, and gestured for her to stand on his other side. Sky took her place and turned to survey the shocked crowd with an impudent gleam in her eyes.

'Well, that was a surprise,' Jewel muttered to Britta. 'That shook the traders' daughters. Almost worth waiting around for, eh, little nodnap?'

Britta could not answer. She had been prepared for Vashti's success, but to see the scornful Sky of Rithmere in the place of honour gave her a sour feeling in her stomach.

'One to go,' said Jewel, and crossed her fingers.

Sorrel cleared his throat. Absolute silence fell. He looked at the card again, though surely it was not necessary, and looked up.

'Jewel of Broome!' he said.

A collective sigh gusted through the room. As Jewel, stiff with shock, moved towards Sorrel, Britta felt her own web of dreams unravel, the frail, vivid threads falling like ash around her feet.

So it is over, she thought dully, making herself clap as Sorrel shook Jewel's hand.

Sorrel began rumbling on about the rules of the Rosalyn Trust, but Britta could not attend to him.

It is just as well I was not chosen, she told herself, looking down at her hands. Think what Mother would have said if I had gained a place!

But she could not help remembering Sorrel bending forward and saying, 'You did very well, on the whole. Very well.' She could not help wondering what would have happened if she had not given Jewel the hint about Mab's last question. Perhaps then Jewel would not have impressed the committee so highly. Perhaps she, Britta, would have been standing there instead …

'Britta!'

The name penetrated Britta's thoughts. Her head jerked up. Sorrel was looking directly at her. As she stared at him in confusion, he beckoned a little impatiently, as if he had called her more than once.

'Make haste, Britta, if you please!' he ordered. 'It is getting on for six o'clock, and a tie in a contest like this is not something that can be settled in a moment. Mab wishes to speak to you and the others. And Mab, as you will learn, does not like to be kept waiting.'

10 - One Gold Coin

It seemed that Vashti, Britta, Sky and Jewel had scored so evenly in both test and interview that it had been impossible to choose between them. It had been decided that there would have to be another test to break the tie.

Clearly Zoolah disagreed, and by the poisonous glances she cast at Britta it was plain which finalist she thought should have been marked down. Mab did not look pleased either, but she seemed merely impatient at the delay. Sorrel was as calm as ever, and it was he who explained what the new test would be.

Each of the four finalists would be given one gold coin, to make a purchase somewhere in the harbour district. A receipt would be required as proof that the trade had been made by the rules. The time limit was two hours. The three finalists whose purchases were judged to be the best value for money would sail on the *Star of Deltora* the following day.

It could not have escaped Sorrel's notice that as he spoke Jewel, Sky and Britta all began to fidget, but he made no comment. He finished his little speech as smoothly as he had begun, then blandly asked if there were any questions.

'I would like to know why the contest is to be held in Del harbour,' Jewel said bluntly. 'Vashti has grown up here. She will have a great advantage over the rest of us.'

'Clearly,' Sky muttered.

Britta said nothing. The final test was unfair, certainly, but she had more worries than that. For one thing, now she would not be starting for home till sometime after eight o'clock. Visions of her mother's panic rose before her eyes.

'I have not come all the way from Broome to fail because of an unfair test,' Jewel insisted, meeting Mab's cold gaze unflinchingly.

Vashti widened her eyes and looked innocent. Zoolah, who had flushed scarlet with anger at Jewel's impertinence, opened her mouth to speak. But before she could say a word, there was a casual knock on the door and a bulky man with coal black skin and a well-clipped pepper-and-salt beard strode into the room. A cap bearing the emblem of the Rosalyn fleet was pulled low over his grey hair, which was tied back in a short tail.

'Please, Captain Hara!' Zoolah snapped. 'We are

in conference and cannot be disturbed!'

Ignoring her, the man looked at Mab. 'You sent for me?' he asked.

'Indeed I did, Hara,' said Mab calmly. 'You and I have things to discuss, and I cannot leave the Traders' Hall at present. There has been a delay. We have four equal scores here.'

Hara frowned slightly. 'If we do not sail with the dawn tide—'

'There is no question of that,' Mab broke in. 'One moment!' She turned to the candidates.

'The situation is not ideal, I agree, but it cannot be helped,' she said, speaking especially to Jewel. 'Time is too short for us to take you to a place where none of you is known. I advise all of you who are strangers here to trust your instincts. A good trader can make a bargain anywhere.'

Nodding curtly to Sorrel and Zoolah, she left the room with the captain.

'So that seems to be that,' Jewel said, speaking to no one in particular.

Vashti cleared her throat. 'I would like to write a note to my parents, if that is permitted,' she purred, fluttering her long eyelashes at Sorrel. 'They were to send the carriage for me at six—'

'Oh, the *carriage!*' Sky muttered.

'—and I would not like them to be worried needlessly,' Vashti went on, as if there had been no interruption worth noticing.

'Naturally!' Zoolah exclaimed. 'Write a note, by all means, Vashti, and it will be sent to your parents at once.'

Sorrel smoothed his moustache. 'Of course,' he murmured, 'as I am sure you realise, Vashti, you must give no details of the new test in the message. There must be no suspicion that any of the candidates has been assisted.'

'I quite understand, Trader Sorrel,' Vashti replied composedly.

'I also wish to send word—to Captain Gripp, if you please,' Britta hastened to say. Inwardly, she was cheering. If she sent a message to Gripp telling him she would be late, he could send Bosun to the shop with a note saying she was safe!

Then she faced reality. Captain Gripp had spent his life at sea. He had no family, and did not understand how mothers fretted about their children. It would never occur to him to send the polypan to the shop unless ... unless, somehow, Britta could put the idea into his head.

The solution came to her like a flash of light. There was a very simple code—part of a treasure-hunting game that she and the captain used to play in the old days. They had called the game 'Gilly's Gold'. Would Gripp remember it?

All she could do was try, and hope for the best. She took the paper and pen Sorrel passed to her and, thinking furiously, scribbled a note:

> Dear Gilly,
>
> They have asked me to stay longer than expected. Will be doing another test. Be assured that I am well. Worried, but well. At least I am still in the running. Home too late to cook dinner. Bosun can do it. Must go. Take care of yourself. Note that the new test is secret. Saying anything about it is forbidden. I will explain later. Am hoping for the best. Safe so far, in any case.
>
> Britta

Inwardly quaking, Britta handed the note to Sorrel. The words sounded so clumsy! What if Sorrel realised that the first word of every sentence was a message within a message?

But Sorrel merely glanced at the note and gave her a brief smile.

'Why have you addressed it to "Gilly"?' Zoolah asked suspiciously, reading the note over Sorrel's shoulder.

'Oh, that is what I have always called Captain

Gripp,' Britta said, hoping her nervousness would be taken for embarrassment.

'And who is this "Bosun"?'

'Bosun is Gripp's polypan,' snapped Sorrel, for the first time showing signs of temper. 'Vashti, have you finished?' He held out his hand.

Vashti signed her message with a flourish and gave it to him. As he scanned it Britta saw it too, and was irritated to see how elegantly written it was compared to her own.

> Dear Mother and Father,
> I will not need the carriage for a
> few hours more because Trader
> Mab has set us another test. This is
> unexpected, but I trust that calm
> and firmness will help me succeed.
> Love and kisses,
>
> *V.*

'Very well,' said Sorrel. 'Zoolah?'

Zoolah opened a small purse and, as reluctantly as if the money were her own, passed one gold coin to each of the finalists.

'Remember, the time limit is two hours and not a minute longer,' she said fussily, turning to look at the clock on the wall. 'It is now … six o'clock precisely. You may go!'

Sky, Jewel and Vashti darted out of the room. Britta hung back a little, and by the time Zoolah shut the door behind her, the corridor was deserted.

Britta walked slowly towards the luncheon room, wrestling with her second problem. The last thing she had expected was to have to trade in Del harbour. With every extra person she spoke to, the danger that she would be recognised became greater.

She knew that her fears were illogical. If she became Mab's Apprentice, she would not be able to skulk and hide. Everyone in the harbour would see her at one time or another.

But somehow this knowledge did not help, and it came to her that by now her sights were set so firmly on sailing with the *Star of Deltora* in the morning that future problems had begun to seem of no importance.

One step at a time, she told herself. My task now is to get aboard the *Star*, and that means I can take no risks. Well, soon it will be dark. If I only visit small shops in the back streets, all should be well. No doubt it will mean buying several cheaper items instead of one big one, but that does not matter—the total value is what counts.

She passed a mirror and glanced at her own reflection. Her hair was falling down around her ears. Her face looked pale and haunted.

I cannot go trading like this, she thought. I look demented!

Not far ahead was the traders' washroom. Britta hurried into it, and found another mirror.

She was combing her hair furiously, preparing to pin it into its usual tight knot, when she realised that the dark waves hanging around her shoulders made a good disguise. No one in the harbour had ever seen her with her hair loose.

Perhaps something could be done about her clothes as well! Quickly she looked around. In a corner of the washroom was a box overflowing with musty-smelling garments. A sign above the box read:

> *For old sailors in need.*
> *All donations*
> *welcome.*

Well, Britta thought, rummaging guiltily through the box, I am not an old sailor, but I am definitely in need. And it is not really stealing. I will return whatever I take as soon as this is over.

Most of the clothes were far too big for her, but at last she found some baggy trousers and a washed-out tunic she thought might fit. She tore off her shirt and skirt and pulled on the shabby garments, trying not to think too hard about who had worn them before her.

A cracked leather belt completed the outfit. When Britta looked into the mirror again, she saw a stranger who might have been the fair-skinned cousin of Sky of Rithmere, but certainly could never be mistaken for a trader's daughter.

Cautiously she left the washroom and in moments was slipping out of the Traders' Hall and making her way up to the harbour streets.

The taverns were becoming rowdy. The smells of fried fish and roasted sweet potato filled the warm, salty air. No one paid any attention to Britta, and soon she was feeling almost light-hearted. It was so much easier to walk wearing trousers instead of her usual hobbling skirt. It was wonderful to be free of the collar that buttoned so tightly around her neck. And how good it felt to have her hair hanging loose, instead of scraped back and held in place by a dozen rigid hairpins!

Turning a corner she glimpsed both Jewel and Vashti ahead. Jewel was looking in the window of a weapons shop called Hotnots & Sons. Vashti was walking into Carme & Furness, a large store that sold leather goods. There was no sign of Sky.

Keeping to her plan, Britta strode on till she reached the narrow back streets. The shops here were small and badly lit, but she did not think the less of them for that. *A Trader's Life* said that bargains were often to be found in dingy, unfashionable places, and her own experience had taught her that this was true.

Not just her own experience, either …

Before Britta could stifle the thought, she was remembering sitting on her father's knee, warm and safe, watching colours and shapes moving inside a shining glass ball. The sky sphere had been Dare Larsett's most prized possession, always kept on his writing desk. It was magical and precious. Yet Larsett had found it covered in dust in a dark corner of a tiny, out-of-the-way shop on the isle of Dorne.

Angrily Britta shook her head, driving the memory from her mind, refusing to admit the pain it had brought with it. The days of her childhood were long gone—gone as surely as her father and the sky sphere. She had to think only of the present and future now.

She began her search, darting into every shop that looked promising and prowling the shelves. The unfriendly stares of the shopkeepers surprised her at first. Then she remembered her shabby clothes, and realised with amusement that the owners suspected her of looking for something to steal.

She saw nothing that was even worth stealing

in the first six shops, but in the seventh she found the treasure she had been hoping for. A small pottery lantern, very simple but beautifully shaped, was lying wedged among some other household goods in a box by the shop's counter. She freed the lantern from the rest of the clutter and examined it carefully.

She had never seen a lantern like it before. It was old, certainly, and grimy with soot. But it could be cleaned, it had no chips or cracks, and there was such beauty in its simple lines that Britta felt in her bones that it had been crafted by an artist.

She became aware that the keeper of the shop, a scrawny man with watery eyes, was watching her.

'How much are you asking for this?' she asked casually.

The man shrugged, peering at the lantern. 'That box was only brought in an hour ago,' he said. 'My sister hasn't been through it yet. This is her shop—I'm just minding it while she's out having her bad leg seen to. You'd best come back in the morning.'

'I cannot do that,' Britta said firmly. 'I am in a hurry. What would you say to two silver coins?'

'I'd say you must be joking,' said the man, a shrewd light suddenly coming into his watery eyes. 'That's a quality lantern, that is. A bit out of the ordinary, too—that's always worth money, my sister says. An' it'll clean up beautiful.'

But Britta could see that he had been bored and was keen to make a sale. Her confidence rose, and after some brisk haggling a bargain was struck.

The harbour clock was chiming seven as she left the shop with the lantern wrapped in an old piece of sacking and plenty of change clinking in her pocket. Feeling elated, she walked on down the dim street, keeping her eyes open for another bargain.

The shops on the harbour outskirts, however, seemed to close earlier than the stores closer to the docks. Many owners had barred their doors while she had been haggling for the lantern. By the time she turned the corner into the next street, there were few people about and it was growing very dark.

Britta began to feel uneasy. Abruptly she changed direction, slipping into an alley that looked as if it led to a busier road. Almost at once she thought she heard footsteps behind her, and her heart beat faster.

Do not be stupid, she told herself. No one is following you! Who would bother to rob someone who looks so poor?

And the next moment feet pounded on the cobblestones and someone sprang at her from behind. Her head exploded with pain. Stars danced before her eyes. Then there was only darkness.

11 - The Cellar

Britta woke with a pounding headache and no idea of how much time had passed. It was so dark that she could see nothing at all. She was lying on hard stones, but she knew she was no longer on the street. The air was cool and stale, and she could smell damp and mould.

She discovered that the sacking package she had carried away from the shop was still wedged in the crook of her arm, and coins still chinked together in her pocket. A stab of surprise was instantly followed by a thrill of dread. If a street thief had not attacked her, who had?

She froze, every nerve straining to detect the slightest sign that an enemy was lurking close by in the darkness. But there was not a breath, not a trace of human scent or warmth in the still, dank air. And it came to her that she could sense no feeling of evil will in the cellar—quite the opposite, in fact. The darkness seemed to press in upon her softly, mournfully, almost as if it were trying to offer comfort.

Telling herself not to be fanciful, Britta crawled to her knees. Her head swam. She felt around blindly. Her groping fingers found the slimy stone of a wall, and using it to steady her she slowly clambered to her feet.

The hair on the top of her head snagged on rough wood, and reaching up to free it she touched heavy beams and rough planks. They are part of the floor of the building above me, she thought. I am in a cellar—below street level. At the same time she saw, on the wall straight ahead of her, a fine, straight line—not of light, exactly, but of less intense darkness. She reached out to it and again felt wood.

She traced the outline of what seemed to be a door in the wall, just below the roof of her prison. With a shock she remembered a similar trapdoor set into the side of her mother's shop, at ground level. It led down to a cavity that was supposed to be for underground storage but was too damp and awkward to be used.

The alley where she had been attacked was the other side of this door, she was sure of it. She had been stunned, then slung into this dungeon like a sack of tarny roots.

She could find no fastening on the door and it would not budge when she pushed it. No doubt it was bolted on the outside. She beat on the wood with her fists and shouted for help, but no one answered her calls.

Of course not. The shops had all closed for the day. The alley was deserted. No one was going to come—at least till morning, and by then it would be too late. For all Britta knew, in fact, eight o'clock had come and gone and it was too late already.

And suddenly, on a hot wave of anger, it came to her that perhaps this was the whole point. If only three finalists returned to the Traders' Hall on time, the contest was over, whatever those finalists had bought. What if she had been locked up simply to get her out of the way?

Britta's face burned in the darkness. The more she thought about it, the more certain she became that her wild idea was right. But which of the other finalists would have done such a thing? Sky? Vashti? Jewel?

The names echoed in her pounding head. She pressed her hands to her temples, closed her eyes, and deliberately slowed her breathing. Into her mind swam some words from *A Trader's Life*:

The good trader always focuses on his or her main aim. It is folly to waste energy in fruitless raging against fate, the weather, or persons who seek to stand in our way. All our intelligence should be directed to gaining the result we want.

It does not matter who did this, Britta told herself. The important thing now is to get out of here!

The darkness pressed in around her. She seemed to hear voices whispering to her, faint and anxious.

There is a way out, Larsett's daughter, the voices seemed to be saying. *You have only to find it.*

Britta knew the voices must be products of the thick silence and her imagination, but she also knew that she could not stay where she was, vainly beating on a trapdoor that would not open.

She began edging along the walls of her prison, patting the stones from floor to roof. Her head was spinning. Her knees trembled. But she kept moving. And at last, at the bottom of the second corner, she found a narrow gap in the stones.

There ... the voices breathed.

Britta did not hesitate. She squeezed through the gap and found herself in a low, narrow tunnel. She did not know why it was there. Perhaps it was a drain that was no longer used. Perhaps the Resistance fighters had dug it in the time of the Shadow Lord. Whatever it was, it was a way out—if she was prepared to squirm.

And squirm she did, trying not to listen to the whispers that crawled with her, trying not to think about where the tunnel might end.

It ended in a glimmer of light—in another underground chamber, many times larger than the one she had left.

Britta slithered gratefully into the new chamber without a thought of danger. Only when she was scrambling to her feet in the dimly lit space, only when she saw a dark figure rise from the floor like a towering phantom, did she feel fear.

'Who are you?' the figure croaked.

Shrinking back, Britta looked around dazedly, her eyes dazzled by the light, dim as it was. She saw a bed of straw, a blanket and the flickering stump of a candle. She saw a battered stove, and a table and stool both made of sturdy wooden boxes. And then she looked higher and saw shelves fixed to stone walls, every shelf crammed with pottery lanterns, exact copies of the one she had bought.

She stared, stunned.

'Why do you not answer?' hissed the voice in the shadows. 'Who are you? Who sent you?'

A gaunt man stumbled into the light and Britta shrank back with a gasp of horror. One side of the man's face was hideously scarred, the skin white, shiny and crumpled, the eye sealed shut. His hands shook violently. His thin lips writhed and twitched as if they had a life of their own.

'N-no one sent me,' Britta stammered. 'I was locked in—back there.' She gestured at the hole in the wall behind her. 'I crawled ... I just wanted to escape! Please—do not harm me!'

'Harm you?' The man stared at her, his lips still twitching. Greasy grey hair hung in rats' tails to his shoulders and his clothes were little more than rags bound about him with string. He pressed his bony hands together, plainly in an effort to stop their shaking, and at that moment Britta realised that he was as frightened as she was.

This does not mean he is not dangerous, she reminded herself, and sidled away from him, looking desperately for a way out.

'You—you have not come to take me to the palace?' the man croaked.

'No,' Britta managed to say.

'I cannot stay in the palace, though our king himself invited me to do so, because I was hurt in the Shadowlands,' the man said, his voice rising as if she had argued with him. 'The healers and nurses are kind and the food is good, but I must be here to finish my task. If I am taken back to the palace I will run away as I did before.'

Britta bit her lip. So this poor man was one of the lost souls she had been thinking about on the way to the harbour yesterday. More than his face had been scarred by what he had suffered during the rule of the Shadow Lord.

She had seen such people in the streets, had even met one or two in her own neighbourhood. But now, for the first time, she truly faced the horror of the time before she was born—the time that had always seemed like a colourful story, exciting but a little unreal. Her father had sometimes spoken of it, but her mother never had. Maarie believed that such things were not for children to worry about, and were best forgotten.

Britta swallowed. 'I understand,' she said slowly

and carefully. 'I am sorry to have troubled you. If you show me the way out, I will go and leave you in peace.'

'Oh, but I cannot let you go!' The man wagged his head from side to side, greasy strands of hair flapping his cheeks. 'You might tell.'

'Tell what?' Britta cried, her chest tight with horror.

'You might tell where I am hiding, so others will come and take me away. Then who would guard the lanterns from theft or harm? I cannot afford to lose even one. There are still not enough. Not nearly enough!'

Wildly Britta tore her eyes from his twitching face and turned to look at the lanterns ranged on the shelves. There were dozens of them!

'I made sixty-one in all, for the Resistance, just before the pottery was raided and burned,' the scarred man whispered hoarsely. 'They were not my best work, for they had to be made quickly and in secret, but they were needed for the Cause.'

He twisted his trembling hands together first one way, then the other.

'In the Shadowlands I dreamed of rescue, but when I returned to Del nothing was as it had been before … before I made the Resistance lanterns. And one night while I lay awake in our good king's shelter, it came to me that if only I could get them all back, get them honestly and cleanly, perhaps my old life and skill would return to me as well.'

Britta's heart swelled with horrified pity. She could think of nothing to say, but the old man did not seem to mind. He went on in a low mutter, almost as if he was talking to himself.

'So I came here to this secret den, where my lanterns were once hidden with other things we did not want the Grey Guards to find,' he said, glancing restlessly at his table and stool. 'The den was as safe as it had always been, as were the hidden treasures, but only five lanterns remained. The Resistance fighters took the rest, no doubt. They are scattered and lost.'

He sighed. 'I search for them everywhere, and trade for them when I find them. All the shopkeepers hereabouts know me, and if one of my lanterns comes into their hands they keep it till I come. They know I will pay well. And every night, when people are long abed, I prowl the streets picking through the barrels of rubbish put out for the carts, for even a broken lantern can be mended. But fewer come to light every year, and so far I have only forty.'

'That is a very large number,' said Britta, her heart beating so hard with hope and fear that she could hardly speak.

'Not enough,' the old man mumbled. 'I must find the rest before I can be at peace. At one time I had a friend who looked them out for me, but he has not brought me one for a long, long while. I fear he has forgotten old Shivers. I do not blame him. He is a busy man, a great man, with many affairs on his mind.'

111

He bent his head. His hair swung forward, hiding his blind eye, his scarred face.

'Master Shivers,' Britta said softly. 'See what I have.'

And slowly, as the old man looked up, she unwrapped her package.

12 - The Bargain

As the sacking fell to the ground, Shivers gave a harsh cry. He reached out for the pottery lantern but, hardening her heart, Britta held it away from him. 'In return for this, you must show me the way out, and let me leave,' she said. 'I will tell no one where to find you, I swear it on my honour.'

Tears were glistening in the man's one good eye. His lips were working, his hands were trembling. Britta wondered if he was going to lunge at her and try to take the lantern by force, despite what he had said about gaining his collection honestly and cleanly. Fighting down her fear, she raised her chin and stood her ground.

'That is a fair bargain, is it not?' she asked.

'No!' Shivers muttered. 'No, no!'

Abruptly he turned and limped to the wooden box that served him as a stool. He lifted the box's lid, felt around inside, then hurried back to Britta with something in his hand.

It was an exquisite pottery candlestick, glazed in glorious sky blue. Britta drew a sharp breath.

'I made only one of these,' Shivers said, pushing the candlestick towards her. 'It was part of the trove hidden here by the owners of the pottery in the time of the Shadow Lord. I offer it, and your release, for the lantern and your promise to keep my secret.'

'It is far too much,' Britta said faintly. 'All I want is—'

'No! The blue candlestick was to be the next trade!' Shivers exclaimed, growing very agitated. 'I decided on that long ago. Bad luck will fall on my quest if you do not take it. The great man who sought lanterns for me would take nothing in return, but that was different. He was rich, and my good friend. You are poor, and a stranger. I must not cheat you. Accept what I offer—I beg you!'

Britta looked at him helplessly. He was in earnest—she could see it plainly. But beside the humble lantern, the candlestick glowed like a star. There was no comparison between the two. One was a useful, well-designed object. The other was—simply—beauty.

And yet ... and yet it was the small, plain lantern the old man wanted. He cared nothing for the candlestick. The lantern was his heart's desire.

So in that way, the trade was fair. And in any case, Britta was certain she would not get away from the cellar unless she accepted Shivers' terms.

'Very well,' she murmured, pulling herself together. 'We have a bargain. Now—'

'Wait!' cried Shivers in high excitement. 'The trade must be official. I must give you a receipt. Wait!'

He scurried away again, rummaged in the table box for paper and pencil, and in a few moments was back with a note bearing a few scrawled words. Anxiously he held it out to show what he had written:

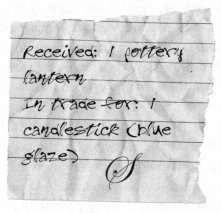

Received: 1 pottery
lantern
In trade for: 1
candlestick (blue
glaze)

'My signature is not what it was, but it will be accepted as my mark, I am sure,' the old man said, with a tiny glimmer of pride. 'I always used to sign my best work in that way—do you see?' Carefully he tipped the blue candlestick, to show the 'S' engraved on the base.

Britta nodded, but did not let down her guard. 'Now lead me out, if you please,' she said, holding tightly to the lantern. 'Then we will make our trade.'

Shivers wrapped the candlestick in a piece of rag and shuffled away, beckoning Britta to follow him. In minutes she was sliding through a trapdoor onto the moonlit cobblestones of a street while he stared after her in feverish impatience.

'Thank you,' she whispered, crouching to take the candlestick and the receipt from him, and handing him the lantern.

The old man pressed the lantern to his scarred cheek in an ecstasy of joy. 'Forty-one!' he crooned. 'Now I have forty-one!' He began to lower the trapdoor, plainly longing to gloat over his treasure in peace.

'Is there nothing I can do for you, Master Shivers?' Britta asked impulsively. 'I swore to tell no one where you live, and I will not. But ...'

'Watch for my lanterns, and if you find another, bring it to me,' the man begged. 'And if you should see my great friend, remind him of old Shivers.'

The trapdoor was now so low that only his good eye was visible, glinting in the gloom within.

'Wait!' Britta cried, crouching to keep the eye in view. 'I will do as you ask, but what is your friend's name? What does he look like?'

A mournful chuckle came from the darkness. 'If you meet him, you will know him at once. You cannot mistake him. He is tall, with eager eyes, hair as dark as yours, and a smile that would charm the fish from the sea. But if you need a name, I will give it to you. His name is Dare Larsett.'

The trapdoor closed with a dull thud.

Stunned, Britta stumbled down the narrow street with no idea where she was. Moonlight flooded the cobblestones. The deep shadows that crawled beneath the awnings of the darkened buildings seemed to whisper the words that were echoing in her mind over and over again. *His name is Dare Larsett. Larsett …*

A thundered curse jolted her violently from her trance. She jerked her head up and in terror saw a powerful figure running towards her.

'Stop!' a deep voice bellowed as she turned to flee. 'Britta!'

Britta knew the voice. And as she checked her flight and turned back, she recognised the shouting man, too. Dark face. Grey-streaked beard. Peaked cap. It was Hara, captain of the *Star of Deltora!*

'By all the serpents and little fishes, girl, what are you doing here?' Hara panted as he reached her side. 'Make haste!'

When Britta hesitated, bewildered, he threw his arm around her waist without ceremony and began to run, half dragging and half carrying her back the way he had come.

Britta did not resist him. She was too shocked by all that had happened to do more than stumble beside him, clutching Shivers' candlestick to her chest.

They turned one corner, then another, and another. Salt breeze beat against Britta's burning face, easing her throbbing head. The sound of water slapping against the sea wall was suddenly loud in her ears.

Then there was bright light ahead and she could hear another sound—the sound of the harbour clock beginning to strike. One … two …

'Come *on*, girl!' Hara roared. 'You can still do it! Come on!'

The truth burst upon Britta like an exploding star. The Traders' Hall, every window blazing, was just ahead. And there was only one way to take what Hara had said. She had not been underground for as long as she had feared. The clock was only now striking eight!

With the last of her strength she flung herself forward, for the first time keeping pace with Hara, no longer holding him back. Now she could see the doors of the hall standing wide open, straight ahead of her, and she made for that golden square of light thinking of nothing else. The chimes of the clock were ringing in her ears. She did not count them. She knew only that she had to outrun them.

Hara was shouting. Britta saw figures appearing in the golden square, looking out at her. She saw mouths open. She heard someone give a high, carolling call.

Then the figures were scattering, and she and Hara were bursting into the light, into the entry room of the Traders' Hall. Mab, Zoolah and Sorrel were there, but in that instant all Britta saw were the faces of her three rivals—Sky grinning, Jewel cheering, Vashti looking disdainful. It came into her dazed mind that one of them must be shocked to see her. One of them had thought she was safely out of the way, locked up in the dark.

But that one, it seemed, was a fine deceiver who could hide her real feelings behind a mask and keep her secrets hidden.

The clock struck for the last time, and the sound of the chime died away.

'Ho, you made a grand entrance this time, little nodnap!' cried Jewel. 'We had quite given you up! But by the stars, what are you wearing? Have you been taking lessons in dress from Sky of Rithmere?'

'She could have done worse,' Sky said. 'She could never have run like that in a skirt.'

'Disgraceful!' snapped Zoolah. 'Why, I do believe those garments came from the old sailors' box!'

'It is not a bad plan to dress plainly when trading in the poorer quarters of a city,' Sorrel murmured. 'Was that your idea, Britta?'

Britta, bent almost double and gasping for breath, did not even try to answer.

'She was in a poor street, certainly, when I met with her,' panted Hara. 'Such places can be dangerous at night. I thought it best to escort her back.'

Zoolah pursed her thin lips. 'I doubt that is permitted!'

'I can think of no rule against it, Zoolah,' Sorrel replied. 'The important thing is that the trade was done without aid.'

Hara shrugged his broad shoulders. 'I know nothing of the trade, but the girl has a package with her.'

'So I see,' Mab said coldly. 'Then I suggest we return to the conference room and make an end of this. Thank you, Hara. I will see you in the morning.'

It was a clear dismissal. Without a glance at Britta, the sweating man turned on his heel and left.

'You seem to enjoy making other people wait, Candidate,' Zoolah sneered.

'I—could not help it,' Britta managed to say. 'Someone knocked me down and shut me in a cellar. It took time to get out.'

She glanced at the other finalists as she spoke. They all looked merely startled. None of their faces showed a flicker of guilt.

'If you were foolish enough to wander the back streets alone in the dark, you deserved whatever you got, my girl,' Zoolah scolded, as Mab scowled and Sorrel exclaimed in concern.

Britta said nothing more. She could see there was no point.

In silence Mab led the way to the conference room. In silence she sat down at the head of the table. The long day had clearly taken its toll on her. Her painted face looked gaunt beneath the crest of bright hair.

She waited, her lips pressed together, while Sorrel and Zoolah took their places on either side of her. Sorrel nodded slightly at Vashti, Sky and Jewel and they slid into chairs at the other end of the table. The tension in the room was so thick that even Jewel did not say a word.

'So, Britta,' said Mab, 'what do you have for us?' She did not sound as if she was expecting a great deal.

Britta limped to the head of the table, her rag bundle still clutched to her chest.

'You should know, Britta, that the other three candidates have excelled themselves,' Zoolah said, gesturing at three differently shaped boxes lined up on the tabletop. 'Vashti secured a splendid carved leather belt worth, by our reckoning, three gold pieces on the open market. The candidate Sky has a box of six mirrored juggling balls that we value at two gold pieces. And the candidate Jewel has matched that figure with a very fine bone-handled knife. It will be hard for you to do better.'

'Thank you, Zoolah!' Mab snapped. 'Britta?'

With difficulty, Britta forced her stiff fingers to release their grip on the bundle. She pulled away the filthy rag covering, put the blue glazed candlestick on the table, and waited.

13 - The Deed

There was a stunned silence in the conference room. 'But—but that is—that is a—a Sheevers candlestick!' Sorrel spluttered at last, his mild, pleasant face flushing bright red in excitement and disbelief. 'From before the invasion! See the Sheevers glaze? It is unmistakable! Why, it must be worth … oh, thirty gold pieces at least!'

'At least,' Mab agreed, gazing at the candlestick in fascination. 'Forty—even fifty to a collector, perhaps, by now.' She looked up at Britta, a strange, startled look in her eyes. 'By the stars, girl, where did you get this?'

'Plainly she stole it,' Zoolah said in disgust. 'How else could she have come by it?'

At the other end of the table, Vashti widened her eyes and made a small, scandalised sound. Jewel and Sky kept silent, but they both leaned forward, watching intently.

Britta shook her head. Suddenly she was so tired that she could hardly remain upright. 'I traded for the candlestick,' she said. 'I had it from the maker—Master Shiv—Sheevers—in return for something he wanted more.'

'Sheevers is dead,' Sorrel said blankly.

'No.' Britta fumbled in her ragged pocket and handed over the old man's receipt.

'Forged!' snapped Zoolah, craning her neck to see the scrap of paper.

'Zoolah, be quiet!' Mab barked. 'You are making a fool of yourself!'

The stout woman flinched as if she had been slapped. Her blunt face went scarlet. Almost, Britta could have felt sorry for her. Almost.

'I do not think this receipt is a fraud,' Sorrel said quietly. 'The writing is unsteady, but the signature is Sheevers'. I have seen it too often to be mistaken.'

He looked up at Britta. 'Where is he?'

'I promised not to tell,' Britta said, barely moving her lips. 'I wish I could, because Master Shivers—Sheevers—needs help, certainly. But I swore on my honour.'

She held her breath.

'Trader Sorrel accepts the receipt as genuine, and so do I,' Mab said flatly, spreading her bony fingers on the shining tabletop and staring down at them. 'The Sheevers candlestick is by far the most successful trade of the evening. The candidate Britta is therefore a finalist in the Rosalyn Trust contest and will sail on the *Star of Deltora* in the morning.'

Britta's knees turned to jelly. It was all she could do not to sink to the ground where she stood. For an instant the stuffy air of the conference room seemed to be swirling with whispering shadows. Then the shadows had vanished, and she was left clinging to the back of the chair for support, but otherwise herself again.

'The candidate Vashti, in second place, is clearly also a finalist,' Mab was continuing, still looking at her hands. She sounded exhausted. Her blue eyelids drooped. The rouge on her cheeks stood out in hectic patches because all the natural colour beneath it had drained away.

Mab is old, Britta thought suddenly. She is old and frail, whatever she pretends. She should have taken an Apprentice long ago, not left it till now, when her strength is waning. Anyone can see that she is sick of this whole affair!

'But what of us?' Jewel exclaimed, glancing at Sky. 'Our trades were of equal value!'

'We have two good candidates,' Britta heard Mab mutter to Sorrel. 'Surely that is enough?'

Sulking in her chair, Zoolah puffed up in outrage, but tightened her lips and said nothing.

Sorrel shook his head. 'I am sorry, Mab. It is inconvenient, I know, but the original rules of the Rosalyn Trust—'

Abruptly he broke off. His eyes bulged slightly and he clapped his hand over his mouth.

'Curse you, Sorrel, what is it now?' Mab barked, clearly at the end of her endurance.

Sorrel had turned bright red again. Slowly he uncovered his mouth. 'I—I think I have remembered something. By the stars, can my memory be playing me false? It is so many years since I—'

'Stop blithering, man!' roared Mab, slamming her hands on the table. 'Spit it out!'

Sorrel pulled himself together. He stood up, smoothed his moustache and walked briskly to the door. 'I am not sure, but I may have the answer,' he said in his usual measured tones. 'I must check. If you will kindly wait … no, no, on second thoughts I would rather you came with me, Mab. You also, Zoolah, if you please. If I am right, there should be witnesses.'

Mab and Zoolah, both holding themselves very straight, followed him from the room. Wondering, Britta and the other candidates crowded after them, in time to see Sorrel unlocking a door a little farther down the corridor.

'The library!' Vashti exclaimed.

Sorrel and Mab hurried through the open door with Zoolah close behind them, her voice raised in shrill, gabbling complaint.

'Why do they put up with that woman?' Sky muttered. 'She is as stupid as an owl, and does nothing but cause trouble!'

'The Trust committee keeps hoping she will retire—she is not in good health—but she will never go willingly, my father says,' said Vashti, with the lofty, irritating air of one who knows. 'She enjoys her little bit of power too much. And they feel they cannot make her go. Zoolah has worked for the Rosalyn Trust since she was a girl. And, of course, her brother was Mikah, the captain who died trying to bring the *Star of Deltora* home.'

Britta felt the corridor shift around her. Dizzy and sick, she swayed as she saw again words carved on a stone in a rain-drenched graveyard.

Foully betrayed by one he trusted …

Someone gripped her arm and pushed her head down a little. The sickness and dizziness passed. She straightened slowly, looked round and saw Sky beside her, eyebrows raised in amusement.

'I thought you were about to entertain us further with a fainting fit,' Sky murmured.

'I am perfectly well,' snapped Britta, pulling her arm free. She bit her lip, instantly regretting her rudeness, as Sky turned away with a shrug. Surely the young woman of Rithmere would not have come to her aid a bare hour after knocking her down and pushing her into a cellar?

She might, if only to cover her tracks, a voice in Britta's mind whispered. *You cannot trust her, any more than you can trust the others. Best keep apart from all of them until you know which one …*

A raucous shout of glee cut through her bleak thoughts. She looked up to see Jewel and Vashti bolting into the library, with Sky close behind them.

Something had happened! Britta moved as quickly as she dared to the open doorway and looked into a large room lined with books. She saw everyone gathered around a table on which lay a shallow wooden box. Above their heads, the portrait of a beautiful, black-haired woman stared icily from a golden frame. It was a painting of the first Trader Rosalyn—Britta was certain.

'Come in, Britta!' called Sorrel, beckoning. 'You may never have another chance to see this, and I must put it back in the vault directly. Too much light will damage it.'

'You should not have taken it out in the first place!' Zoolah scolded. 'It should never be removed from the vault! Never!'

Mab snorted. 'If it can never be seen by human eyes, what is the point in keeping it? It survived many years out of the vault at the time of the invasion, Zoolah, not to mention two long sea voyages—and it can survive five minutes now.'

Britta caught her breath as she reached the table and saw what lay inside the box. It was an ancient parchment, sealed under glass and signed 'Rosalyn' in a bold hand.

'Yes.' Sorrel nodded, regarding the document reverently. 'This is the original Trust Deed, penned by Rosalyn herself. I have seen it only once before myself—when I removed it from the old Traders' Hall to save it from the enemy. I was only eighteen—many years ago now.' He smiled ruefully.

'Look here, little nodnap!' Jewel cried, pointing to some lines about two-thirds of the way down the page.

Slowly Britta read the faded words:

𝕿𝖍𝖊 𝖍𝖎𝖌𝖍𝖊𝖘𝖙 𝖘𝖈𝖔𝖗𝖎𝖓𝖌 𝕮𝖆𝖓𝖉𝖎𝖉𝖆𝖙𝖊𝖘, 𝖙𝖍𝖗𝖊𝖊 𝖆𝖙 𝖙𝖍𝖊 𝖑𝖊𝖆𝖘𝖙, 𝖆𝖗𝖊 𝖙𝖔 𝖇𝖊 𝖙𝖆𝖐𝖊𝖓 𝖔𝖓 𝖆 𝖙𝖗𝖆𝖉𝖎𝖓𝖌 𝖛𝖔𝖞𝖆𝖌𝖊 𝖎𝖓 𝖙𝖍𝖊 𝖋𝖎𝖓𝖊𝖘𝖙 𝖘𝖍𝖎𝖕 𝖔𝖋 𝖙𝖍𝖊 𝖋𝖑𝖊𝖊𝖙 ...

'You see?' Jewel exclaimed. 'The original Deed says there must be three finalists *at the least*, not three finalists *only*. So all is well! Four finalists are not unlawful! We can all go! All four of us!'

'Indeed. Two of you will have to share a cabin, that is all,' Mab said.

There was a short, stiff silence. No one looked at anyone else.

Jewel was the first to recover. 'I have no objection to sharing,' she said cheerfully, looking round at Vashti, Sky and Britta. 'Though I warn you, I snore!'

'Then Vashti, Britta and I will decide between us who shares with you,' said Sky, without hesitation.

'Why not?' cooed Vashti, narrowing her blue, slanted eyes.

Jewel grimaced. This, plainly, had not been her

idea at all when she had confessed to snoring.

Britta's chest tightened. She had very good reason for wanting a cabin of her own, but so far she had said nothing about suspecting one of the other finalists of attacking her, and she was reluctant to raise the matter now. It would complicate everything. The voyage might even be delayed while Mab and Sorrel tried to find out who the culprit was.

And delay, Britta decided, was to be avoided at all costs. She was a finalist—she had got what she wanted. She could deal with the matter of the cabins when the *Star of Deltora* was safely at sea.

'So that is settled,' said Mab. 'Four finalists it is.'

'There have always been *three* finalists,' Zoolah argued in a high voice, as if doubting the evidence of her own eyes. 'All the record books say—'

'For centuries, certainly, the number has been kept to three,' Sorrel broke in patiently. 'No doubt it began as a matter of convenience, because private cabins are few on most trading vessels. Then it became tradition, and the original wording of the Deed was forgotten. I had forgotten it myself until a few minutes ago, and even then I was not sure. It was just the faintest wisp of memory.'

'A pity it did not waft into your mind a little earlier,' Mab remarked tartly.

Sorrel shrugged. 'Indeed! But in my defence, the actual wording of the Deed was of no real interest to me at the time I saw it. Being male, I had always known

I could never hope to become the Trader Rosalyn, however long and faithfully I served the fleet.'

No edge of bitterness sharpened his voice, but looking at him keenly, Britta wondered how he really felt. It suddenly occurred to her that her father had had good reason to leave the Rosalyn fleet and begin an independent trading life, quite apart from his thirst for adventure.

Still . . .

She glanced up at the beautiful woman in the portrait. She met the strange, painted eyes, and felt they were boring into her own. She wondered what sadness—what tragedy, perhaps—had driven all warmth and life from those eyes. And she felt selfishly, profoundly grateful that the Trader Rosalyn had reached down through the centuries and held out to a girl with nothing but hope this chance, this amazing chance, to gain her heart's desire.

Thank you, she said to the portrait silently. And then, as Sorrel returned the Trust Deed to its vault, Zoolah brooded and Mab offered Jewel and Sky beds in the Traders' Hall for the night, Britta tore her mind from the past and began busily to plan.

She could farewell Jantsy at the bakery in the morning, on her way to the ship. For tonight, she must recover her own clothes from the washroom, tell Captain Gripp of her success, hurry home, pack for the voyage and . . .

And break the news to her mother.

14 - Beneath the Stars

Midnight had come and gone, but time had little meaning on the black-rimmed Isle of Tier. The island had engulfed a drifting ship and was slowly feeding. Slight tremors rippled its surface as it consumed sodden timbers, ragged sails, rotting bales of silk and the bodies of crew long dead of plague. In the centre, the being who was once a man sat as always. Sometimes his mind idled, but for many years now true sleep had eluded him.

Wraiths whispered around his golden throne. The black diamond Staff stood under his hand, its tip buried deep in the soil of the island's heart. A waterfall of emeralds poured out its wealth beside him, but he did not regard it. It had pleased him when he first created it, but it bored him now.

Britta is your daughter, Larsett, Master of the Staff! the wraiths whispered. *She is blood of your blood, bone of your bone. Why did you not tell us?*

A hundred times the wraiths had asked this since they returned, flitting like grey mist over the darkened sea. If he did not answer, the whispers would go on and on, and the pictures of what the wraiths had seen in Del would continue to flicker among them. The hand on the Staff tightened, and relaxed.

'Yes,' the King of Tier said aloud. He gazed at the images dancing in the air before him—Britta staring at a gibbering polypan, Britta writing at a table, crawling through a tunnel, running with a dark, burly man, placing a blue candlestick on a polished table. 'She is my daughter. Why should this surprise you? You know what I gave up to bring the Staff to you. Stand back! It is not your business to question me!'

The wraiths retreated, cowed by his anger. But they watched him, watched him closely and he knew it, though he pretended otherwise.

'Setting sail in the morning,' he murmured. 'With Mab, on the *Star of Deltora*. A finalist in the Trader Rosalyn contest ... I had not thought of that.'

Emeralds piled in drifts around his feet as he pondered what the wraiths had shown him. Mab, fierce as ever, still clinging to power while her body failed her. Natty Sorrel, not a dark hair left on his head. Zoolah, grown stout and troublesome. And Britta, no longer a child but a determined young woman with her father's eyes.

With an impatient gesture the King extinguished

the emerald fountain, which collapsed into dust.

'But what does it matter, after all?' he mumbled. 'She will not come here. The oceans are wide. Tier is well concealed. And by now she has surely forgotten, as I had almost forgotten ...'

But as he rested his heavy head on his free hand, the foreboding that had plagued him for days returned, rolling over him like a thundercloud.

The wraiths who had been away from him so long slid closer, anxious, worshipful.

'Go back to her!' he snarled. 'Do not return till you know where the ship is bound. I must know more!'

The wraiths moaned, and left him.

Far across the dark water, beneath the same cold stars, Britta was fleeing from her home, a bundle of belongings slung over her aching shoulder.

She had parted from her mother in anger. Wild with shock, hurt and rage, Maarie had said everything she could think of to make her daughter give up the chance of sailing on the *Star of Deltora*. She had called Britta wilful, disloyal and ungrateful. She had cried that Britta was cutting her to the heart—and in that she spoke the simple truth.

But Britta had expected opposition, and had steeled herself to resist it. After hours of argument, she had retreated into hard silence. Tight-lipped, she had tied what she needed for the voyage into a shawl, ignoring both her mother's frantic attempts to stop her and Margareth's silent misery. Still without speaking, she had clattered down the stairs to the kitchen, dragging her bundle behind her.

'I will tell them!' Maarie had shouted, running after her and clutching her arm. 'I will tell Mab whose daughter you are! That will end this madness!'

But Britta had known the threat was empty. Her mother would never dare to make a fuss that would draw unwelcome attention to the little shop in the city's centre. Her expression must have revealed her scorn, because Maarie, white with rage, had lashed out and slapped her across the face—slapped her for the first time in her life.

'Go, then!' Maarie had shrieked, for once too furious to consider gossiping neighbours or anyone else who might be listening outside. 'Break my heart, like your father before you! I wash my hands of you!'

And Britta, her cheek hot and tingling, her head held high, had seized her bundle and her shabby cloak and swept out into the night without a word. As the door slammed behind her she had heard her mother burst into a storm of passionate sobs, but she had not turned back. She had shouldered her bundle, hurried along the shop's narrow side passage to the street and set off towards the harbour, seething with anger.

She walked defiantly and fast in the middle of the road, the anger blinding and deafening her to everything but her own thoughts. If a figure slid silently after her, keeping to the more complete blackness of the road's edge, she was not aware of it. She had covered some distance before she noticed light, running footsteps behind her.

She spun round, ready to fight. And there was Margareth, panting, her face wet with tears.

'Go back, Margareth!' Britta snapped. 'I will be quite safe. Captain Gripp will be glad to give me a bed for the night. He, at least, is proud of me.'

She clung to the memory of her last, rushed visit to the warm little house on the harbour. She relived Gripp's shout of joy as she burst in with her news, his raucous, loving congratulations, his delighted guffaws as he boasted of understanding the note addressed to 'Gilly' and acting upon it at once. Even Bosun the polypan, quite recovered from whatever had ailed him on Britta's previous visit, had happily capered and hooted about her, sharing in the celebration.

'Do not feel bitter towards poor Mother, Britta,' Margareth pleaded. 'She loves you dearly. She is hurt, and afraid. She did not mean what she said.'

'She did,' Britta retorted. 'She meant every word of it. And as for loving me—she does not love me as I am! She only loves the girl she thinks I should be—a good, quiet, home-loving girl like you. But I cannot be like you, Margareth! I do not even want to be!'

She saw her sister wince, and felt a sharp pang of remorse. 'Oh, that came out wrongly! I did not mean—'

'I know,' Margareth said softly. 'Britta—'

'I cannot give this up, Marthy!' Britta broke in, unconsciously using the old pet name she had given her sister when they were children. 'This is my chance—my only chance ...'

'I know,' Margareth said again. 'I did not come after you to beg you to return, Britta. I just could not bear to let you go so hurt and angry. I wanted to say goodbye, and ...'

She pulled from her pocket a little coin purse embroidered with birds and flowers. 'I finished this last night,' she said, pressing the purse into Britta's hands. 'It was supposed to be your birthday present, but then Mother became ill and I had to put it aside, so it was not ready when it should have been. In any case, it is done now, and I wanted you to have it. I hope it will bring you luck.'

Britta could not speak. She flung herself into her sister's arms and hugged her tightly.

'Keep safe, dear Britta,' she heard Margareth murmur against her cheek. 'Keep safe and come back to us.'

And then with a sob Margareth was pulling away and running back up the street.

Britta lifted the purse to her lips before putting it carefully away in the buttoned pocket of her skirt with her notebook, her pencil, her comb and the clean handkerchief her mother had taught her to carry always. And then she shouldered her bundle again and walked on, towards the harbour.

The anger that had made her blood race had ebbed away, leaving her merely numb. Even when she reached the shuttered bakery and realised that now she would not be able to say goodbye to Jantsy, she felt very little.

She tore a page from her notebook and wrote a few lines.

> Jantsy—I won a place on the Star of Deltora and am sailing with her at dawn. Mother is very angry, so I am going to Captain Gripp's to sleep. I am sorry to leave without saying goodbye, but your parents would not like it if I knocked so late. The voyage will take about 12 weeks. Take care of yourself.
>
> B.

Britta pushed the note under the bakery door. Then she wrapped her cloak more tightly around her and trudged on. She had not the slightest inkling that at this moment shadows whispering her name were rushing towards her over black, heaving water. She did not think of Jantsy, her mother or Margareth. She did not notice the soft night air on her skin, or see the lights of the palace glowing against the sky, or feel the need to look up at the stars. And she did not sense the enemy creeping after her in the dark, gloating and triumphant, burning with ill will.

She felt nothing at all. She just walked, her mind a blank, her eyes on her feet. She simply walked and walked until at last the streets she trod were the streets of the harbour district, and she tasted salt on her lips, and the harbour clock was striking three not far ahead.

'So your attendants have left you, my pretty,' a voice croaked beside her.

Starting violently, Britta looked round. Just visible in the dimness crouched a bone-thin woman with an embroidered shawl over her head.

'Did you bid them go on some errand? Or did they go of their own accord?' the woman asked, her eyes great, dark pools in her lean face.

Britta's heart was thudding wildly, but she managed a shaky smile. This woman, no doubt, was like Sheevers—another poor soul whose mind had been scarred by suffering.

'I think you are mistaking me for someone else,' she said gently. She began to move on, but a thin hand, the fingers heavy with rings, shot out and caught the edge of her cloak.

'Listen to Lean Alice!' the woman hissed. 'The boy would not listen to her, but you surely must! If you have power over your spirit attendants, you should call them to you now. Ill will follows you. It is very near, and will destroy you if it can.'

'I—I am sorry,' Britta gasped, dread causing her voice to catch in her throat. 'I—I do not understand you. Please let me go!'

And then boots were tapping on the cobbles, the thin woman was shrinking back with a gasp, and a far heavier, stronger hand was seizing Britta's wrist, twisting it spitefully.

'So!' a horribly familiar voice shrilled in Britta's ear. 'An orphan, are you? A distant, worthy relative of that lying villain Gripp, are you? How is it, then, that you have a home and family in the centre of Del?'

And Britta spun round to meet the glittering, triumphant eyes of Zoolah.

15 - Ill Will

The shock was terrible. The wave of sick dismay that quickly followed it almost made Britta sway where she stood. Zoolah's face was so full of gleeful malice that it looked like a painted mask. Her upper lip was curled up almost to her flaring nostrils, baring gums as well as teeth.

'I followed you when you left the Traders' Hall, Britta—or whatever your true name is!' the woman jeered. 'I saw you go into Gripp's hovel, but I waited, just in case. And sure enough, barely ten minutes later, out you came again, peering about you like the cheat and fraud you are. And off you scurried to a wretched little shop in the centre, to a mother who screeches like a fishwife and a sister who runs about the streets in her house slippers, blubbering like a child.'

Anger flared in Britta, driving the hot blood into her face, stiffening her spine. 'Shut your mouth!' she hissed. 'They are both worth ten of you!'

'Ha, now you show your true colours!' cried Zoolah. 'You mimic the dress of a trader's daughter but you are no lady! I knew that! I knew it the minute I saw you, with your impudent eyes, your cheap, mended shirt flapping and your hair falling about your ears! Better a savage from Broome or a Rithmere pauper than that, I thought!'

She drew a deep, shuddering breath. 'But Mab would not be told, or Sorrel either! I knew you must have cheated in the test, though I had not seen you do it, but they would not listen when I told them so. At the interview they gave you a value far beyond what you were worth, and when I argued, they insulted me!'

The rage in the high, trembling voice made it only too clear what had driven Zoolah to follow Britta through the night, and to skulk in the dark for hours behind the little shop in the centre. It was not spite against Britta alone, but rage because Sorrel and Mab had ignored the views of Zoolah, Senior Management Officer of the Rosalyn Trust. Fury caused by injured pride was at the root of all Zoolah had done.

It was horrible, and its result was devastating, but through Britta's misery ran a single thread of relief. Plainly, Zoolah had not guessed who she was. Zoolah had no idea that she had beneath her hand the daughter of the man who had caused Mikah's death.

And she must not find it out, Britta thought frantically. No one must find out. For Mother's sake.

141

For Margareth's sake. If people discover who they are they will have to move again, run away again, hide again. They will lose the shop and everything they have built. Because of me.

She felt sick as she realised fully how she had endangered her family's security by her reckless pretence. Her mother had tried to tell her, but she had not listened. Consumed by her own burning hopes, she had risked the safety of those she loved best in the world on a gamble—a gamble she had lost.

I will not let them be hurt! Britta swore to herself. Whatever it costs me, I will find a way to protect them. She looked at Zoolah with hatred. The woman's glee was nauseating.

'Now Mab will see how right I was!' Zoolah was crowing. 'When I tell her what I have seen with my own eyes and heard with my own ears she will have no choice but to call the guards and have you taken in charge! And she and Sorrel will listen to me the next time, oh yes!'

Her grip tightened and she began to march Britta on down the street as if she were a guard herself. Without actually hurting her, Britta could not break free, and there was no point in escaping anyway. Zoolah knew about the shop, and would surely rush back there, plunging Maarie and Margareth into a nightmare, if Britta ran.

Think! Britta ordered herself. *Think!* And then the answer came to her.

'It is not a crime to be poor, Zoolah!' she almost shouted. 'It is not even a crime to lie, in a matter such as this. But it was a crime when you hit me and pushed me into that cellar, during the final test! It was a crime when you locked me in, so that I would be late to the Traders' Hall! *Those* things were crimes, Zoolah, without a doubt!'

Zoolah glanced at her blankly, but kept moving.

'If you let me go free now, I swear I will not be at the dock tomorrow when the *Star of Deltora* sails,' Britta said. 'Mab and Trader Sorrel will think I was afraid to go on the voyage, and forget me. I will never trouble you again! But if you take me to Mab now, Zoolah, I will tell! I will tell everyone what you did to me! And *you* are the one who will be taken in charge!'

'What nonsense is this?' Zoolah jerked her head as if ridding herself of an annoying insect. 'I did nothing to you! During the final test I was having dinner in the Traders' Hall. Mab and Sorrel were with me. They know that I never set foot outside.'

'Then you hired someone else to attack me!' But even as Britta spoke she knew she was clutching at straws. Zoolah would never have risked her reputation by hiring someone who might later tell of what she had done.

Zoolah smiled without humour. Sweat dripped from her mottled face and stained the neck and armpits of her tight, high-necked jacket, but she did not slow for an instant.

'I have committed no crime, girl!' she jeered. 'But *you* have! Cheating and lying in Del's most important contest may not be against the law of the land, but thieving is! And you are a thief! How else could a chit like you lay hands on a Sheevers candlestick?'

'Master Sheevers gave it to me in trade for a lantern!' Britta cried. 'You know it! You saw his receipt!'

'Liar!' Zoolah spat. 'Sheevers is long dead! Everyone knows that!'

She started violently as a thin face loomed up beside her and long fingers heavy with rings plucked at her sleeve.

'Shivers is only dead to the world, fine lady,' a panting voice rasped. 'He walks, breathes and speaks like you or me.'

'How dare you follow us, vermin?' Zoolah shrieked. 'How dare you touch me? Get away!' She kicked out viciously and with a groan Lean Alice crumpled onto the cobbles.

'Oh, she is hurt!' Britta shouted, struggling to break free and go to the fallen woman's aid. 'You have hurt her! Zoolah, let me go!'

But Zoolah paid no attention. She set off again, faster than ever, pulling her captive with her.

'Beware, fine lady!' Lean Alice croaked after her. 'I warn you! The girl has dealings with the dead in body, as well as the dead in spirit. I have seen them with her in this very street, attending her, fawning upon her, watching and listening. They have left her for now, but at any moment they may return. You would do well to let her alone!'

Wheezing and blowing, Zoolah hurried on.

'Fine friends you have, indeed, Miss!' she gasped. 'Lean Alice—your accomplice in thieving, no doubt! Wait till I tell Mab and Sorrel of this!'

'Lean Alice did nothing!' Britta cried. 'She—'

'Still, I did see you slide a note under the door of that bakery,' Zoolah went on, following her own line of thought. 'Perhaps your accomplice works there. And then there is Gripp! Yes! Gripp keeps a polypan, and polypans steal as easily as they breathe! Well, the guards will find out the truth of it.'

They turned the last corner, and then the harbour itself was before them. The rising tide slapped heavily against the sea wall. The Traders' Hall was a dark, imposing shape not far away. At the end of the silent graveyard, the little shelter under which Britta and Jewel had taken refuge from the rain was silhouetted against the sky. In the *Star of Deltora*, rocking at her mooring, a single light glowed.

Britta could not see the hands on the harbour clock, but she knew that the night—this terrible, ill-omened night—was coming to an end. Already the water was high. Just before dawn the tide would be at its peak. And then, as the sun rose, the tide would turn and the *Star of Deltora* would set sail—with Vashti, Jewel and Sky, but without Britta.

So there will be only three finalists after all, Britta thought drearily. A burning lump rose in her throat, but her eyes remained dry.

Listlessly she stumbled with Zoolah down to the Traders' Hall. The best she could hope for now was that Mab would accept her apology, believe that Captain Gripp was somehow not to blame for the lies, and let Britta go without calling the guards or pursuing the matter further.

As Zoolah rapped at the door of the Hall, Britta tried to think of the words that would gain her what she wanted. But she was so tired! Her mind was spinning—whether as a result of the blow to her head or as a result of all that had happened to her since, she did not know. For some reason, the words cried after Zoolah by the old woman who called herself Lean Alice kept coming back to her.

The girl has dealings with the dead in body, as well as the dead in spirit. I have seen them with her in this very street, attending her, fawning upon her, watching and listening ...

What had Lean Alice sensed to make her say such things? The talk of the walking dead was of course merely frightening nonsense, but ... but perhaps the woman was truly psychic. Perhaps she had seen into Britta's soul—seen that Britta was so haunted by her past that she seemed surrounded by shadows.

Suddenly Britta longed to go back, to find Lean Alice and ask her to explain. But by now the fortune-teller would surely have crawled into some place of safety where she could not be found. And Zoolah, impatient, was rapping at the door again. In a few moments Mab would come. After that, even if the very best happened, Britta would never dare to come to the harbour district again.

There was the sound of a bolt sliding back, and the door opened a little. The soft glow of lantern light seeped through the narrow gap. A sturdy woman in a white nightgown, her cropped grey hair standing on end like a brush, glared out.

Zoolah puffed out her chest. 'Healer Kay,' she shrilled. 'It is I, Zoolah!'

'Keep your voice down, for pity's sake!' the woman in the nightgown whispered. 'Zoolah, what do you mean by knocking at this hour?'

'I must see Trader Mab at once!' Zoolah said hoarsely. 'It is a matter of the greatest importance.'

Raising her eyebrows, the healer spared Britta a brief glance before turning her attention back to the feverish woman in front of her. 'Mab is asleep,' she said flatly. 'Your business will have to wait.'

'It cannot wait!' Zoolah insisted, pressing forward. 'I must see Mab now, this minute!'

The healer stood her ground, shaking her head. 'Mab is asleep, I tell you! She needs her rest, and I will not allow her to be woken earlier than necessary.'

She peered more closely at Zoolah's swollen, sweating face and her frown deepened. 'You are not well, Zoolah,' she added in a different tone, again glancing briefly at Britta. 'I strongly advise you to go home and get some sleep yourself.'

Zoolah bared her teeth. 'You are not my healer!' she hissed. 'I do not take orders from you! Stand aside!'

'There is no question of that,' Kay said calmly. 'If you will not take my advice, that is your own affair. As you say, I am not your healer. But I *am* Mab's healer, and you are not seeing Mab tonight, Zoolah—make up your mind to it.'

Zoolah charged forward. She was strong, but the healer was stronger, and ready for her. With a furious gasp Zoolah staggered back, pushed none too gently by the flat of a broad, capable hand.

'You will regret this, Kay!' she choked. 'You will regret it to the end of your days!'

'I doubt it,' the healer said. She nodded at Britta. 'Who is this?'

Zoolah spat at her.

'Very well!' Kay's grey eyes hardened. 'Go home, Zoolah! Or stay here and wait till dawn if you wish. But I warn you, if you beat upon this door again, or make any further rumpus, I will summon a guard to remove you. Do you understand?'

She stepped back and closed the door in Zoolah's face. The bolt slid home with a firm click.

16 - Shadows

For a long moment, Zoolah simply stood where she was, staring at the closed door. She was breathing hard and fast. It seemed to Britta, watching numbly, that her enemy's colour was coming and going, one moment mottled scarlet, the next fish-belly white.

Then abruptly Zoolah turned and made for the graveyard, hauling Britta after her like a lump of driftwood she had found on the shore. Panting and muttering under her breath, she kicked her way through the sea daisies till she reached the little shelter by the sea wall. And there she flung herself onto a bench, wrenching Britta's wrist until the girl was forced to crouch on the ground at her feet.

'So, now I know where I stand!' Zoolah said aloud. 'Enemies are all about me! But they will learn their error soon enough. When Mab hears what I have to say she will dismiss that impertinent healer from her service, you mark my words. And you need not think, girl, that this delay will profit you one jot!'

'I am far from thinking that,' Britta retorted, and she spoke no more than the truth. If Zoolah had been able to see Mab at once, at least the meeting would have been almost private. By dawn it would be a different story.

Jewel and Sky were sleeping in the Traders' Hall, and they would be up and around at first light, preparing for the voyage. They would hear everything, and the word would soon spread—to Captain Hara on the *Star of Deltora*, to Vashti, arriving at the dock with her parents, to Trader Sorrel, come to farewell the finalists he had helped to choose. They would all be there to witness Britta's disgrace.

And what if ... Britta shivered. What if Mab changed her mind about the Sheevers candlestick? What if, finding that Britta had lied about so much else, Mab began to believe Zoolah's claim that the candlestick was stolen?

Then the palace guards would come. They would question Britta. Her only way of proving her innocence would be to lead them to Sheevers' hiding place. And that she could not do. She had sworn that she would not betray the old man—sworn it on her honour, as part of a solemn bargain. It was a promise she could not break.

The rising water was noisy against the sea wall,

150

and the timbers of the docks were creaking. So neither Britta nor Zoolah heard the footsteps plodding slowly towards them through the dark graveyard. They only realised they were no longer alone when two ragged figures loomed up beside the shelter, one behind the other, like spectres newly risen from their graves.

Zoolah screamed piercingly, thrust Britta at the threatening figures and flung herself onto the tabletop, scrambling across it and tumbling to the ground on the other side. Picking herself up, she backed away till she was pressed against the sea wall and could go no farther.

Britta's throat had closed in terror, but as she leaped to her feet the first of the figures spoke.

'Do not fear. You know me. I have brought the one you need to save yourself.'

The figure bent forward, and with astonishment Britta recognised the embroidered shawl and thin face of Lean Alice.

'Make use of him quickly,' the fortune-teller said in a low, rapid voice. 'Your attendants are returning, I feel it, and I have no wish to see them again.'

'M-my—attendants?' Britta stammered, a chill running down her spine. 'What do you—?'

Shaking her head Lean Alice stepped aside. Behind her, twitching and trembling, was a gaunt, stooped man with a blind eye and a cruelly scarred face. Britta's heart gave a great thud.

On the other side of the table, Zoolah screamed

again and again. Her hands were pressed to her crimson cheeks. Her eyes, fixed on the scarred man, bulged with terror.

'Zoolah, be still!' Britta cried angrily, seeing the old man shrink back. 'It is only Master Sheevers. He will not harm you!'

'Sheevers?' Zoolah's jaw dropped.

Lights had begun to go on—in the *Star of Deltora*, in the Traders' Hall, in the great houses that faced the water and the humble cottages on the shore. Soon people would come running, in response to Zoolah's screams.

'Master Sheevers!' Britta said faintly. 'How—?'

'Shivers comes by my corner most nights,' Lean Alice broke in, seeing that her companion could not bring himself to speak. 'Tonight he came and found me hurt. I told him that the enemy who harmed me had accused you of thieving. He made me lead him to you. He did not want to come here, and nor did I, but he said … he said it was his duty to speak for you. He said he owed it to one who had been a true friend to him.'

'A true friend, he was!' croaked the ragged old man, suddenly finding his voice. 'He helped me often and often in days gone by. He has forgotten old Shivers now, but Shivers has not forgotten him. When I said his name I heard the girl gasp. And then, puzzling it out in my den, I saw what I should have seen before. Her hair … the shape of her face … the eager light in her eyes ... the things she said to me ...'

'Master Sheevers!' Britta cried, glancing in fright at Zoolah, who was goggling at them, her mouth still hanging open. 'I understand! Do not say any more!'

But it seemed that Sheevers, having begun to tell his story, could not stop. 'And I knew!' he crowed, his face writhing, his hands twisting together as if they had a life of their own. 'My friend had a daughter—two daughters—but the younger his very image! Yes! He told me that, often and often. And it came to me that I had just met her—met her and traded with her, all unknowing! The daughter of Dare Larsett!'

Again the air was split by Zoolah's scream, not a cry of fear this time, but a shriek of pure hatred.

'Larsett's daughter!' she hissed, staring with loathing at the girl standing frozen on the other side of the table. 'Of *course*! His older child was Margareth! The younger was—was *Britta!* I should have known who you were the moment I heard your name, the moment I saw your impudent face!'

Her breath was coming fast and hard. Her pudgy fingers had curved into claws as if she longed to leap at Britta and seize her by the throat. 'I even heard the clues, falling from your miserable mother's mouth and from your own. But you did not say your father's name, and how could I have guessed it? Everyone believes that Larsett's family fled from Del!'

Larsett ...

The name seemed to echo in the air. The wind

was rising, sweeping in from the heaving sea. Britta could see bobbing lights beyond the graveyard, and hear the shouts of running people.

'Here!' shrieked Zoolah, her voice cracking. 'Help! Make haste!'

She began to cough, choking and gasping. Spray spattered her head and shoulders as the sea slapped the wall behind her, but she seemed not to feel it.

'How did you dare to show your face at the Traders' Hall?' she hissed at Britta. 'How did you dare, you worthless chit, knowing what your evil father is, and what he has done?'

Sheevers gazed at Zoolah in bewilderment. Lean Alice cringed, her great eyes fearful, her fingers making strange signs in the air.

'I am not my father!' Britta heard herself say.

'You are his spawn!' Zoolah was shaking from head to foot. Her cheeks were mottled red, purple and white. 'His pride and wickedness were the death of my brother, the noblest and most gallant of men, and that same pride and wickedness runs in your veins! Your cursed father is out of my reach, but you—'

She broke off abruptly, her eyes wild as they glared past Britta, Sheevers and Alice into the darkness of the graveyard. Britta spun round. Lights dipped and swung among the graves, moving ever closer to the shelter.

'How fitting!' she heard Zoolah rasp. 'How fitting that fate has delivered you into my hands here, in the place where my poor brother lies! Hear me, daughter of Larsett—'

Larsett … Larsett … The name seemed to pant eagerly in Britta's ears, borne on the gusting wind from the sea. As she turned back to face her enemy, she heard Lean Alice moan.

Zoolah was nodding, nodding, her draggled hair plastered to her head, her fists pressed to her heaving chest. 'I know you now, Larsett's daughter! Soon every man, woman and child in Del will know you too. I will see to it! But that is not all!'

Her thin lips stretched wide in a ghastly, humourless smile. 'I will see to it that your mother and sister, your bakery henchman, the lying villain Gripp, this pair of beggars you have bound to your service, are exposed for what they are. Never will they have another peaceful moment. I will not rest until they are all harried out of Del with nothing but the clothes on their backs! I swear it, on my brother's grave.'

'They come!' Lean Alice wailed. 'From the sea! From the sea!'

There was terror in her voice. Britta looked past Zoolah, out over the harbour, and all at once it seemed to her that she could see shadows rushing towards her across the black, heaving water.

People carrying lanterns and flaming torches erupted from among the graves and stopped dead at the sight of Sheevers, Lean Alice and Britta facing the glaring, panting Zoolah.

'What is happening here?' a woman demanded. 'Zoolah, calm yourself, for pity's sake!'

Dimly Britta registered the crisp voice of Healer Kay, but she did not turn. She could not tear her eyes from the ragged, speeding shadows. She was waiting for them to vanish, like the illusions she knew they must be—illusions created by fear, by exhaustion, by the mad cries of Lean Alice.

But the shadows did not vanish as they came closer. Instead, as Britta watched, transfixed, they seemed to gather together to form a dark mass that surged towards her, the speed of its passing whipping the surface of the water beneath it into foam.

My mind has created this image, she told herself wildly. My own mind has made me a picture of the horror that is about to break over my head and over the heads of everyone I love.

'Stay away from me, Healer!' Zoolah ordered, light from Kay's lantern flickering crazily over her wet face. 'I have something to say, and I will say it! I will not be silenced!'

She jabbed a shaking finger at the people who had run to her rescue and now stood awkward and staring. 'You are my witnesses!' she cried to them. 'You are my—'

'Beware, lady!' Lean Alice howled.

And Britta screamed as the great, humped wave of darkness burst over the sea wall.

Zoolah, threats still spilling from her mouth in a

vicious stream, was engulfed. Her would-be rescuers fell, roaring with shock, beneath a tumult of foam. Lanterns and torches sizzled and went out. Alice and Sheevers dropped to their knees, clinging together. But Britta stood upright and safe, panting and trembling in the centre of swirling, loving darkness.

17 - Dawn

The small crowd watched silently as Healer Kay laboured to revive the woman sprawled by the sea wall. 'It is no use,' Kay said at last, standing up wearily and wiping sweat from her forehead. 'Her heart will not beat again. The shock when that freak wave hit was too much for her.'

As some of the watchers moved to carry Zoolah away, the healer drew Britta aside.

'Do not blame yourself for this death,' she said in a low voice. 'There was nothing you could have done to stop it. Zoolah's heart has been in a dangerous state for a long time. Her healer, I know, advised her to keep herself calm, but she could not do it. She took offence very easily, poor soul. Well, you witnessed one of her rages tonight.'

Britta shivered, remembering Zoolah's swollen, mottled, hate-filled face.

Kay eyed her keenly. 'Some say it is wrong to speak ill of the dead,' she went on. 'I think it is worse for the living to feel guilty for no reason. Zoolah was one of those people who are obsessed with their own importance and cannot bear to be crossed. Life being what it is, such folk are doomed to be frustrated.'

She grimaced. 'I am only sorry for what you must have gone through after I locked the door of the Traders' Hall against you both. But my thoughts were all for Mab, and you looked … capable.'

Britta nodded soberly. Already what she had seen and felt after the shadowy wave burst over the sea wall had come to seem like a nightmare born of shock and terror. There was no one to tell her differently. By the time the confusion had died down, Lean Alice had vanished with Sheevers.

'You are one of the finalists for the Rosalyn Apprenticeship, are you not?' Kay asked in her abrupt way. 'The one Zoolah did not care for?'

Again Britta nodded. She could not find the strength to speak.

'Mab told me about you,' said the healer. 'You went out with one gold coin and came back with a Sheevers candlestick. Zoolah was convinced you had stolen the treasure, because Sheevers was dead, but if I am right, the old man who was here earlier was Sheevers himself. I saw him once when I was young and I knew him, though he is much changed.'

This time, Britta managed to find her voice.

'He came to speak for me,' she said. 'But—but what happened scared him away. I would be grateful if you could tell Mab that—that you had seen him.'

The healer smiled briefly. 'Mab seems to have no doubt at all that your trade was an honest one, but I will tell her. And now, Britta, I prescribe for you a hot bath, a light meal, and a little sleep. The Traders' Hall guest apartments can supply all you need. Come along! There is no time to waste!'

The news that in defiance of long tradition there were to be not three but four rivals for the Trader Rosalyn Apprenticeship had caused much excited comment in Del trading circles. When the *Star of Deltora* set sail, the dock was packed with curious, chattering onlookers despite the early hour.

The sudden death of Zoolah, Senior Managing Officer of the Rosalyn Trust, had also caused a flutter. But though the people on the dock clicked their tongues and spoke of the tragedy with proper gravity, not one truly mourned. Nor did anyone blame Mab for departing as planned, leaving Trader Sorrel to see Zoolah buried with proper ceremony. Everyone knew the importance of trading schedules.

Later, many would go to Zoolah's funeral and listen gravely as Sorrel spoke of Zoolah's life and work, her many good qualities and her loyalty to the Rosalyn Trust. Some would even shed tears, but the tears would have more to do with their sadness at the passing of time, or their memories of others who had died, than because Zoolah was no more.

Strangely, the person who thought of Zoolah the most that morning was the girl Zoolah had hated and tried to destroy. Standing in the ship's stern with Jewel, Sky and Vashti, Britta found herself looking for a portly, bustling figure among the members of the Rosalyn Trust committee who had come to see the *Star* depart. But of course Zoolah was not there.

Do not blame yourself for this death, Healer Kay had said, and Britta did not—not really. She could not help thinking, however, that if she had never crossed Zoolah's path, never heard of the Rosalyn contest or entered the Traders' Hall, Zoolah would have been alive to revel in this day.

But then I would not be here, Britta thought, her hands tightening on the ship's rail. Jewel, Sky and Vashti would be sailing on the *Star of Deltora*, and I would be waking now in my bed at home with nothing to look forward to but another day in the shop.

Trader Sorrel was on the dock, right at the front. As the band of water between the ship and the land broadened and the faces in the crowd became smaller and less distinct, he was still easy to see, his silver hair gleaming, his arm raised in farewell.

Britta lifted her hand to him. It was mainly to Sorrel, she was sure, that she owed her place on the ship. Without him, she would surely never have scored highly enough to compete in the last test. She remembered vividly how Mab's face had hardened at the mention of Sven's book during the interview. This morning, Mab had been equally gracious to all the finalists as she welcomed them aboard, but it seemed to Britta that there had been no warmth in the old trader's eyes when they met her own.

Well, I have twelve weeks to earn Mab's respect, Britta told herself. And I will do it! I will show her and everyone else that Sorrel was right to support me.

But the thought seemed to echo thinly in her mind as if it were coming to her from somewhere far away. The creaking of the ship's timbers, the splash of the water and the shrieks of the seabirds also seemed strangely muffled. She was rigid with tension, half waiting for a sudden flurry of movement on the dock, for shouts to Mab that one of her finalists was the daughter of a traitor. Even now, there was time for a rowboat to reach them, for Britta to be ordered off the *Star of Deltora* in disgrace.

She glanced at her companions with envy. Vashti, Jewel and Sky were free to relish their success and look forward eagerly to the contest to come. None of them had anything to fear, anything to hide. One of them, certainly, had tried to put Britta out of the contest, but as there had been no witness to the deed there was no real danger of discovery. No one on board carried the burden of a great secret, as she did.

Later, she was to remember that thought with a

rueful smile. For now, it was bitter.

The sails filled above her head, the ship began to move faster. And still there was no angry shout from the dock, no boat sent in pursuit. Britta's tension eased. It looked as if … as if all was going to be well. She watched the land slipping farther away with the sense that she was living in a waking dream. Strange shadows had begun flickering at the corners of her eyes. Blaming the morning glare, she tore her eyes from the dock and looked down.

This moment was not as she had imagined it. Her dearest wish had been granted, but her feelings were very mixed.

Staring sightlessly at the water roiling below her, Britta pressed her hand to her skirt pocket and felt the shapes of the purse, the comb, the notebook, the pencil and the handkerchief beneath the drab blue fabric. Suddenly she felt unbearably lonely.

It came to her that she had chanced everything on this. If she did not succeed, she could never go home. Not after what her mother had said. She could not creep back to the shop, beaten, with her tail between her legs. She would never escape again.

Escape, she thought, focusing on the word that had drifted so naturally into her mind. Is that what I am trying to do? Escape a life that bores and stifles me? Yes. But …

But she had not wanted to escape everyone and everything she loved as well.

She barely noticed the first time Jewel dug her in the ribs. It took a second dig before she looked up.

'Someone is hailing you, little nodnap!' Jewel said, jerking her head to the right. 'See? Over there!'

Britta looked to one side and a lump rose in her throat as she caught sight of two people standing by a little cottage on the harbour shore. One was bent, bearded and leaning on a stick. A polypan capered around him, turning somersaults. The other ... the other was dressed all in white. His honey-coloured hair tossed in the wind. He was waving a red scarf with one hand. The other hand was cupped beside his mouth.

'Good luck, Britta! Good luck!' The shouted words floated to Britta's ears, faint as a distant seabird's cry.

Britta waved wildly to show she had heard. The lump in her throat was burning. After finding her note, Jantsy must have flown through his work and left the bakery the moment it was done. How fast had he run to reach the harbour in time to see the ship sail?

'You will be missed, it seems,' said Jewel, grinning beside her. 'Ah, what it is to be loved! Is that baker's boy your cousin, little nodnap?'

'No,' Britta snapped. 'He is—a friend.' And she tossed her head, ignoring Sky's quick, dark glance and Vashti's supercilious smile.

'A very *good* friend, I would say,' teased Jewel.

Britta did not answer. Her eyes were fixed on the shore, fixed on the white-clad figure that was still resolutely waving its scrap of scarlet.

Goodbye, Jantsy. I will miss you. Goodbye!

She thought the words as if somehow their echo would reach Jantsy's mind. Her heart seemed to have swollen in her chest, spreading warmth through her whole body. The numbness that had dulled her senses had lifted. Her feeling of loneliness had gone.

Now she could feel the fresh wind on her face. She could taste the fine salt spray on her lips. The deck of the *Star* was smooth beneath her feet. The great sails were swelling above her head.

The dock was far behind them now. The people swarming there looked as small as ants.

'Ah!' cried Jewel. 'Look, Britta! We are almost out of the harbour! We are on our way!'

And Britta realised that for the first time in eight long years she was her own person, free of the burden of her father's disgrace. No one on the ship knew who she was, and now there was no way they could find out. She felt the rags and tatters of her past loosen and blow away in the wind.

Whatever the future may hold, she thought, for now I am free! She gave a final useless wave to Jantsy and Gripp, whose figures by now were lost in the distance. Then she turned her back on the land and looked ahead at the wide, glittering sea.

DON'T MISS THE NEXT SPELLBINDING ADVENTURE
IN THE *STAR OF DELTORA* SERIES!

BOOK 2: TWO MOONS

Aboard the *Star of Deltora* with her three rivals for the Trader Rosalyn Apprenticeship, Britta knows that she has to keep her wits about her. She desperately wants to win the contest, but of course Jewel, Sky and Vashti feel the same, and one of them, she knows, is a ruthless enemy who will stop at nothing to succeed.

Britta is ready for trouble, but as the voyage fails to go as planned, and rumours of evil magic sweep her beloved ship, she starts to wonder if she has more to fear than simple human wickedness.

And nothing can prepare her for the terror that awaits her in the perilous, forbidden swamplands of Two Moons.

AUTHOR'S NOTE

Deltora is a place of magic and mystery, but the island it shares with the Shadowlands is only one of the many strange isles that dot the nine seas. Some of the nine seas islands are large, and some are small, but they all have their own rich history and their own stories. I have told a few of these stories already—perhaps you have read them, or will read them sometime in the future.

The five *Rowan of Rin* books are set on an island that lies west of Deltora, across the Silver Sea. Deltorans call Rowan's island 'Maris', because for centuries they have traded with the fish-like Maris people who live on the coast.

One of Rowan's adventures also takes him on a quest to the nearby Land of the Zebak, a dangerous isle where trading ships never go. And somewhere beneath the waters of the Silver Sea is the lost Isle of the Four Sisters, where Flora, Viva, Aqua and Terra still sing to those who have ears to hear them.

The *Three Doors* trilogy is set on Dorne, a small, rich island in the Sea of Serpents, to Deltora's east. Dorne is not only a popular trading port, with many links to Deltora, but also the native land of the magical Fellan. Their mysterious forest surrounds the walled city of Weld, where Rye, the hero of the *Three Doors* story, begins his quest to find his lost brothers.

And then there is *Deltora Quest* itself—the tale of Lief, Barda and Jasmine's heroic struggle to free Deltora from the Shadow Lord's tyranny.

As those who have read *Tales of Deltora* will know, there are hundreds of islands in the nine seas. And there are thousands more stories to tell. I can't promise to tell them all, but sailing with Britta on the great trading ship *Star of Deltora* will certainly give me the chance to try.